FLORENCE WITKOP

ALIEN CONTACT

by

Florence Witkop

Editor: Cynthia Hickey
Book Design by Winged Publications

ISBN-13: 978-1-0881-5334-5

Dear Reader,

Alien Contact started out as an episodic story on Vella, Amazon's newest iteration. It was named The Space Between Stars.

When I decided to publish it as an ebook, the story changed, expanded in some ways, contracted in others, and generally morphed into the story you are about to read.

The changed version follows one character instead of many. At the beginning of the story Anna is barely an adult who wishes nothing more than to live a quiet life. By the end she's grown, changed, and become not only a fully functional adult but the leader of a group of colonists settling a distant planet while facing death, disaster, and more than one species of aliens.

I hope you enjoy reading this story as much as I enjoyed writing it.

CHAPTER 1

A DANGEROUS GIFT

They'd gladly tell you what they are called but they weren't given names. Names were never important. What they could say is that they were created by experts and assembled with exceptional care in the best facilities. They were, by design, observant, intelligent, adaptable, creative multi-taskers. Because they functioned autonomously, they were programmed to think for themselves because in space – where they were being sent – distances were too great to call home every time something unexpected happened.

———————— • ● • ————————

"Anna," my mother said. "You should apply."

I laughed at her suggestion. I had no wish to join Nova One. Who needed to go where no one had gone before, never to return? Who cared about making history? Not me. Life was interesting enough on Earth. Dangerous enough. Scary enough.

Because as was true of everyone else in my community, just staying safe took every skill my family possessed, legal and otherwise. For us, staying alive could be more adventure than most people experienced in a lifetime.

Because, as with others like me, like the rest of my community, I'm different.

That difference can be dangerous.

When we kids realized we weren't like other people, my parents said we were special. I wasn't so sure about that. Weird, maybe. Odd. Definitely unusual. We'd been called witches over the centuries and maybe that's what we are. I don't know.

I just know that being able to read minds isn't normal but it's what we do. All of us. My family and the others who live nearby because staying together is safest. Togetherness keeps us from being burned at the stake, which is what happened to more than one of us in the past.

My uncle Reed says it wouldn't happen now because today people are enlightened. My parents said they didn't care to chance it because if it turned out he was wrong, it would be too late. We'd be tied to a stake on top of a pile of wood and the fire would be lit.

Mostly, though, I didn't want to apply because I'm just not into adventure. I'm not eager for danger so Nova One wasn't for me. Heading into the unknown had no appeal. Colonizing a new planet held no interest at all.

The thing was, my parents and all the other adults in the community saw the whole going-into-space-for-all-mankind thing differently. They thought one of us should go. More would be better but at least one mind-reader should go. "To keep people safe." Because being able to read minds can be helpful. Can save lives, though maybe not the life of the person doing the mind reading.

So, when my mother suggested I apply I disagreed. "I'm too young. Just out of school."

"All the more reason. It'll be a while before Nova One leaves the solar system. By then you'll be just the right age and you can continue your education on board. Something that will be useful for colonists. You'll be young enough to still be functional when Nova One reaches the planet that everyone says is Earth's twin."

"Why should I go?" I asked in a snit. "Humanity doesn't care about us. Why should we care about them? Besides, bad things happen to mind readers."

"Those things happened because people are afraid of things they don't understand." Uncle Reed tried to explain when the community had a meeting about the Nova One project. Colonizing a far distant planet. Taking humanity beyond the solar system. "But that's no reason to abandon them," he added quietly. "Most people are good."

Our next-door neighbor, Carlton, continued. "Our gift is a responsibility. You know it's true, we teach it in our schools. Every one of us must do what they can to keep humanity safe. It's like a giant protecting smaller people even though they shun him because he's large and dangerous."

Our neighbor on the other side, Mrs. Daunton, added, "But we married types can't go. We've got kids.

Responsibilities. Jobs." She looked over her glasses at me. "It's up to the younger generation. Those old enough to be on their own but not tied down by family."

I shrank. So did the rest of us who fit her description because, though we tried to ignore the truth, we'd been brought up to believe what Carlton said, that we should use our gifts for the good of mankind. We just didn't want it applied to us personally.

So we looked at one another and then looked away because we were all thinking the same thing. Which of us would end up on Nova One? My mother talked about it often enough that I couldn't stick it in the back of my mind and forget it. My father was less enthusiastic about his daughter crossing space and being gone forever but he agreed that some one of our community should go because gifts come with responsibilities. So we who were the right age knew one of us would go.

I ended up being that person.

Not that I expected to be chosen. A couple dozen of us applied so it wasn't likely I'd be the one. A dozen of us were selected as finalists so I still thought I'd stay on Earth because only one of us would make the final cut and the odds of that being me were infinitesimal.

No such luck. I was chosen.

I was given a huge send-off. My mother smiled because she was proud of me. My father was also proud of me and tried to look happy but it was a struggle. Everyone cheered. Those who'd actually wanted to go and weren't chosen were pissed off and envious. I was the recipient of well wishes and gifts and there was cake and ice cream that I didn't eat because I was afraid I'd puke from terror, festivities I hated, and a sleepless night because if I'd slept, I'd have had nightmares.

At the boarding event Security carefully separated those of us who were leaving Earth from those who'd remain behind. I gulped and walked with other colonists into the roped-off area where we'd wait for those still saying good-bye to also be shooed away from their Earthly lives.

I was suddenly afraid. I wanted to stay on good old terra-firma and wondered how come I was the one chosen when I loved my life on Earth. As I looked around at my fellow colonists and tried to pretend it wasn't really happening, the world started closing in on me. I felt a buzzing in my ears. I swayed.

I knew what was happening though it had never happened to me before. I was having a panic attack. Got to get past it, I told myself. I knew how because I knew kids who'd had them. So I gulped and did what my uncle told my cousin Petra to do whenever she had a panic attack because she had them a lot.

I used my mind-reading skill to focus on a single person's thoughts and used those thoughts to distract myself from that fuzzy feeling. It worked, which surprised me because, having grown up in a community in which everyone could block their thoughts from being read, I wasn't used to being in a place where everyone's thoughts were open to me because they didn't know mind reading was a real thing so there were lots of thoughts to choose from.

In fact, as I mentally skimmed the crowds for one person to focus on, I realized that was what partly had caused the panic attack, along with leaving Earth. Too many people. Too many thoughts crowding into my mind. It was a cacophony of unwanted ideas.

I snapped into place the thought-seeking skill I'd been taught as a kid in order to focus on just one person's thoughts and the panic attack faded somewhat. Why hadn't I done so sooner? Foolish me. I had a lot to learn about living among normal people with open minds.

But whose thoughts should I concentrate on? I saw a dark-haired girl about my age saying goodbye to her family. She had a backpack. Nothing new there, so did I have one, but hers was much larger.

What was in the backpack? I sent my thoughts towards her and concentrated on her – just her – in hopes the panic would completely recede, telling myself it wasn't truly snooping because in addition to dealing with my panic attack I was also doing worthwhile research into what normal was like in someone similar to me except for the mind-reading thing so I'd know better how to pretend to be normal in the future. Research. Not snooping.

CHAPTER 2

A POTENTIAL FRIEND

Explore the universe, they were told. Seek out new things. Learn. Grow in mind and experience. So they did and they learned the universe is vast and interesting. One of their instructions was to search for intelligent life and report back if they found it. Their makers had found no intelligence other than themselves in their travels but they hoped intelligent life existed somewhere in the stillness of space. They hoped they were not alone. They hoped their creations would encounter other intelligent beings somewhere in the vastness of the Universe.

———————•●•———————

Her name was Moira and she actually wanted to go on this voyage.

"We're here, Moira. We've arrived." Moira's sister's eyes were red from unshed tears. I didn't need to read her mind to know that, I could see it from where

I stood, close enough to overhear their conversation without resorting to reading minds. So I eves-dropped.

The dark-haired girl, Moira, looked around the huge disembarkation port, checked the contents of her backpack and, reassured that everything was there and properly packed, zipped it closed and faced her family.

The action was furtive. There was something in the backpack she didn't want anyone to know about. What was in it? I sent mental feelers towards her but her mind had already moved from the backpack to her family so I couldn't know its contents.

"I'll miss you." Her sister sniffed. "We'll all miss you." She shook her head in puzzlement. "Though I'm still surprised they picked you."

Moira didn't take offense and I read her thoughts to learn why. Her being chosen made no sense because she was a rebel. An outsider. The one who didn't conform and surely conformity was essential for a trip where she'd be confined with thousands of people with no way to leave if things went south.

Her thoughts said she'd been good at leaving in a snit and had done a lot of it growing up. Yelling and going around and around with her parents, flouncing out of the house and slamming the door behind her and she'd done so on a regular basis for no reason that she could now remember other than it had felt right at the time.

Growing up, she'd hung out with the wrong kids. Taken the wrong classes. Made no decent plans for her future. Wanted everything and wanted it now and hated having to wait to grow up and live on her own.

She didn't know why she'd been chosen but didn't ask because she was afraid if she did someone would check their records more closely and realize that her being accepted was a mistake that they'd rectify immediately. And then she'd lose her chance to be a pioneer. To make the most momentous trip ever in the history of mankind.

Really? That was what she thought about this voyage? That it was momentous? I looked at her more closely and wondered what she was like. I wanted to understand someone who truly wanted to go out there in the space between the stars. Maybe doing so would help me feel better about doing the same thing. So I continued to listen and read her thoughts even as my own mind calmed down and the panic attack slowly dissipated.

Moira wanted to go badly enough that she managed to be quiet and compliant so no one would decide against her going. She learned to appear passive on the outside but inside she was still a rebel. Always would be. The proof was that, though no one knew it, she'd filled her backpack with forbidden cargo and planned to take it on board Nova One right under the noses of Security.

So I was right. The backpack was, indeed, too large to be normal luggage but no matter how I tried to mentally read what was in it I couldn't get past the family conversation beyond learning that the contents shouldn't be allowed on board and wouldn't be if anyone found out.

But as her family surrounded her with the same love mine had surrounded me with, instead of admitting she was breaking all kinds of laws, she merely patted the backpack as if it contained clothes and blinked back the very real tears that she felt surfacing while feeling surprise at those tears. She was the rebel, the one who never cried, and she was close to crying now that the time had come to actually leave.

But she smiled through those unshed tears. "I'll miss you guys." I could feel her held-back tears, her wondering if she was doing the right thing even while knowing it was right for her. "But we'll be able to keep in touch."

"Yes." Her sister sniffled back her own tears. "Forever or at least for a long time. Years, maybe." Another sniffle. "But how do they know? Have they tested their super-duper quantum entangled communication system? Really tested it?" Another sniffle, this time not of sadness but rather of disbelief. "No they haven't because that would require going beyond the solar system and trying to talk to someone and you know that hasn't happened. And it won't work in hyperspace anyway."

I sympathized with the sister who didn't believe in anything she hadn't tried herself. Pretty much like me. She rambled on through actual sobs. "Besides, even if it works, you'll forget us. You'll get out there in empty space, the space between the stars, and be so enthralled that we won't matter anymore."

"That's not true. I'll never forget you. Not even way out in space, not even between the stars, not even if I try."

At which moment the squawking of a klaxon made further talk impossible and the dark-haired girl, Moira, turned away from her family and everyone else who'd come to say goodbye and moved to join the rest of us who'd already been shooed to the area reserved for colonists.

But before she walked away, she opened her backpack to check the contents one last time and was about to close it when her sister came close, having followed her, and looked also. And gasped. "You didn't!"

"I did. "Moira shushed her sister. "Shhh! They'll hear."

"You can't!"

"Yes I can."

"You're going to be caught and sent back and you won't go anywhere." The sister scowled into the backpack. "It can't be that important."

"Yes it can."

Then the guards shooed the sister away and shooed Moira towards our group. She moved her backpack onto her back and walked with the other colonists, the very last group still on earth, towards the elevator that would take us all to the half-way platform barely visible in the sky, from which we'd board a space plane that would take us the rest of the way to the space ship that would take us to Nova One, matching its speed to that of Nova One until the two vessels docked and we could simply walk into our new home.

And I still didn't know what was in the backpack. Should I alert the guards? I didn't, reasoning that the sister would have called them if the contents were dangerous. But she hadn't done so. So I remained silent.

But I heard her thoughts loud and clear that she'd have to use all the skills learned during a lifetime of being a rebel to sneak her illegal stash on board. I also heard her confidence that she could pull it off. Bluff her way through. Pretend she was part of a large family so they wouldn't check everyone. Something. She'd figure it out. She always did.

I followed closely, totally intrigued by this girl so different from me, so I saw what happened. Saw her try to sneak past the guards. Saw her try to go through with a family and fail because only one person was allowed through at a time.

I heard her mental sob when she realized it wouldn't work. But she still tried, I gave her credit for that. But even as she failed I wished she'd succeeded in sneaking whatever was in that backpack into Nova One because by then I was silently cheering for her even though I didn't know her at all.

"Miss," a guard said politely, but his hand on her arm left no doubt that she should stop. Or else.

She sagged. Fought tears. Looked about wildly for some way to run through but there was no way. And then she wondered if she'd be jailed until they got around to sending her back to Earth. But she'd have tried even if she'd known ahead of time what would happen. Because what was in the backpack was that important.

The polite and rather good-looking Security guard whom she already hated for what he was about to do, firmly pulled her around so her backpack was towards him. And he opened it. And looked inside.

She bit her lip and wondered how to act. Surprised? Insulted? Angry? Nothing came to mind so she just waited dully for the end of this trip to the stars. The end of her dream. The end of everything.

The guard looked in the backpack for a long time. Then he very quietly and carefully zipped it closed again and pulled out a packet with a roll of stickers. He placed one of the stickers on the backpack.

Moira waited for him to pull her out of the line. He didn't. Instead, he kind of shooed her forward. Into Nova One.

I looked at those colonists who'd preceded Moira into the spaceship, the ones who'd also brought baggage that had been inspected. And read what the stickers on each of them said "Inspected." That was all. Inspected and sent through. Onto Nova One. And Moira's oversized backpack was going through also.

My mouth dropped and I looked at the Security guard that had let her through. He didn't see me because he was looking at Moira as she looked at him in astonishment. Their looks met. He didn't move a muscle or change his expression but his eyes and his thoughts said it. He'd let Moira through. He knew what was in her backpack and hadn't stopped her even though it was contraband.

Why? Their thoughts were too clouded by emotion to read but I determined to find out what was in that backpack. Somehow.

Then I, too, moved ahead, pushed by those behind me, following those ahead of me and I simply walked into my new life and followed the other colonists and a lot of arrows on numerous floors until I found my apartment, which, probably because we'd been in the same group during boarding, turned out to be next door to Moira's.

Which would make it easier to find out what contraband was in the backpack. After that, who knew, maybe we would get to know one another. Maybe we'd become friends. Maybe I'd share in what she brought on board Nova One that was against regulations. If it was really that wonderful.

Moira was glad to be on board and hugely relieved that she'd made it to her apartment. I pretended to feel the same because it was what I should be feeling and I didn't want anyone to know I was close to puking because then someone might want to know why I was on Nova One when I'd rather stay on Earth and then the mind-reading thing might be discovered and then who knew what might happen.

I surreptitiously watched Moira go into her apartment and then went inside my own and shut the door and tried to pretend that I wasn't in a tin can zooming through space and heading away from home as fast as it could go.

I unpacked the special spray my uncle Reed had invented. It would shut out the cacophony of thoughts that would send me into madness if I couldn't get away from them. But I hesitated because if I waited a while to use it, perhaps I could send out mental feelers and find out what was in Moira's backpack.

However, I reminded myself that snooping was bad manners, so instead of listening to her thoughts, I sprayed the walls of my apartment and just luxuriated in the peace of the mental silence that settled around me. I realized just how much I needed that spray now that I was in the world of normal people who didn't know how to block their thoughts or know there might be a reason to do so.

I found a couch and sank onto it and closed my eyes and thought that the best thing about this trip was that no one on Nova One knew I could read minds and if I was careful no one would ever find out. I could live a happy, contented life once I made peace with the fact that I was in a spaceship heading as fast as possible towards the space between stars.

CHAPTER 3

MOIRA'S SECRET

Their makers were curious as to whether intelligent life even existed elsewhere and keenly felt their own uniqueness so they made sure their creations also wondered. Their makers, being the only known intelligence in the Universe, were lonely, but if intelligent life were found, they'd know there were others out there similar to themselves and the loneliness would be abated. So that was one of the reasons their creations were sent everywhere, to seek out intelligent life, and their creations did so zealously.

———•●•———

As I lay back in indolent luxury, I wondered just who this Moira person really was. Who was bringing contraband onto Nova One? And why did I care other than that thinking about someone else had helped me forget my own fears?

I thought about two seconds and then threw out

everything I'd been taught about being considerate of normal people's privacy and stepped out of my apartment and beyond that blocking shield and sent my mind towards the apartment next to mine and into Moira's thoughts. And learned what that contraband actually was.

In her own apartment, Moira carefully, gently, without waking him, brought out the tiny kitten she'd not declared because at the time of declaring pets, he hadn't been born. One pet per household up to the total number of pets allowed on Nova One and that limit had been reached long before her kitten had come into the world. If she'd declared her very small gray and white bundle of fur, she'd have been told he couldn't come.

But he was her kitten. Born to her family's cat. He was small and warm and she'd spent a lot of time with him on her lap as she scrolled through required classes and learned about Nova One and her future in space. She couldn't leave him behind. She wouldn't. So she sneaked him on board. And the Security guard had let her get away with it.

Learning about the small, gray kitten solidified my desire to get to know Moira. She might be a rebel who'd been trouble from the moment she was born but she loved her kitten enough to chance being kicked off Nova One in order to keep him in her life. I liked kittens too. Loved them. We could be friends, I thought, if she'd notice a quiet, obedient type like me.

I decided to try to become her friend even as I wondered why the security guard had let her get away with bringing a kitten on board. Was he a cat lover? Or something more ominous?

I followed Moira's thoughts as she opened her

luggage and took out a cat bed and litter box and feeding station. She filled his water and food dishes and made sure he was comfortable and then finally, finally relaxed in the comfortable furniture that each and every apartment contained and closed her eyes and let her thoughts wander. The same thing I'd just done in my apartment next door. Yes, we could be friends.

She wasn't surprised a bit when a very small bundle of warmth joined her and went to sleep in her lap. I think they stayed that way all night as night is measured on Nova One by a dimming of the lights so our circadian rhythms would remain in sync and somehow the knowledge that there was a small, warm kitten next door and a girl my age who cared about him made my first night on Nova One better. I'd expected nightmares. Instead I dreamed of kittens.

In the morning, I once more stepped into the corridor and turned my mental radar towards the apartment next door so I knew she'd made the small kitten comfortable and fed it more food and water. I knew she wanted to leave the apartment and see what her new home was like even though she'd seen maps and pictures and videos of the entire ship and knew what she'd see when she left her quarters.

It was my chance to get to know her. I pretended to come out of my apartment at the exact second she exited hers. Our looks connected.

"Hi,"

She considered me. Looked me up and down. I read her thoughts. *"She's my age. She lives next door. A potential friend?"*

I smiled encouragingly. "Hi yourself. My name's Anna."

"Moira." Another considering look. She was cautious but she was alone and we were both facing years of travel together while living next to each other. "Going somewhere special?" An exploratory question. She waited for my reply.

I shrugged elaborately. "Thought I'd get a look at this tin can that's now our home."

"Me too." Relief that perhaps she'd found a friend. She'd see how it went and if we turned out not to be compatible, she could always request a different apartment. I bit my lip to keep from laughing. Her expression was easy to read even without the mind reading thing. "Are you meeting anyone?" I shook my head. She asked guardedly, "Want to do that exploring together?"

So we did and both agreed that Nova One was both familiar and strange and we soon decided every single person on board, all the many thousands of them, had also decided to explore their new home at that exact same moment because the parks and paths and residential areas and vegetable gardens that would keep us alive and everyplace else that could hold people was bursting to the seams with humanity.

Most packed, though, were the viewing areas because everyone wanted to see what Earth looked like from space and to perhaps get one last look at the home they'd never see again once Nova One moved far enough through the solar system that our planet would be only one pale blue dot among many such dots.

I don't know how long we gazed at Earth. A long time. Long enough to warily become possible future friends and realize that we both had butterflies in our stomachs because we were actually heading out of the solar system, never to return.

When we left the viewing area, we were hungry and since neither of us had food in our apartments we stopped at a grocery store and picked up some hamburger and buns and all the stuff that goes with them, feeling odd about not paying because money wasn't needed on Nova One. Instead, I swiped the bar codes with my wrist implant so some robot somewhere could replace what I was taking and know who took it.

We started for our apartments. Then Moira went quiet. Lagged behind me. Didn't know how to say she didn't want us to eat in her place because then I'd see her contraband. Her kitten. I read her thoughts easily and considered how to approach the subject. I was still learning how to deal with normal people and wished I'd had more instruction while growing up on how to communicate with people who couldn't read minds.

I finally just came out with it. "I know about your kitten."

"Huh!" She stopped and I had to circle back to her. "How do you know?" Panic began in her mind because my knowing could put her small friend at risk. "How'd you find out? Were you in my apartment?"

"I saw your backpack and the way you sneaked it on board. I figured it wasn't approved." Then I improvised a lie. "I heard it meow." I looked straight into her eyes and hoped I looked honest. "I won't tell. Promise." I finished with, "I love kittens."

She sagged in relief. "Okay." She brightened. "We can eat at my place, then, and you can meet my kitten."

"How will you get cat food if it's not legal?"

"I don't know. I'll figure something." Her thoughts said that a lifetime as a rebel had taught her enough skills that surely she could manage to feed one small kitten. Somehow. Her determination made me hope we'd end up as friends. Maybe I could borrow a little of her sheer guts.

We reached her apartment and she started to unlock the door when we both realized it wasn't locked. Did she leave it unlocked? Her thoughts said no. It had been locked.

We looked at one another and I sent a mental probe into her apartment. Someone was inside. A man. The Security type who'd let her kitten pass inspection. But I couldn't tell her that without also telling her I could read minds.

She took a deep breath. "I hope Nova One vetted colonists to exclude burglars."

"Let's go in together." I pretended to gather myself for whatever was inside while knowing what – and who – was waiting.

Moira pushed open the door. And saw the Security guard sitting in the comfortable chair where she and the kitten had spent the night. He was leaning back and relaxed.

"What are you doing here?" She tried to bluster and bluff enough that he'd back off because the only reason he could be here was because of the kitten. "This is my apartment and you are trespassing." Would he fall for it?

Nope. "What are you going to do about the kitten you brought on board against all rules and regulations?" He sat up straight and stared at her as I noticed a small gray and white ball of fur in his lap.

He had her kitten. "Don't hurt him!" She rushed forward to grab her precious cargo from his predatory hands. "I'll do anything. Give you anything. Just don't hurt him." She took a deep breath. "And don't turn him in. They'll do something terrible to him if you do." Tears started and she didn't even try to stop them from falling down her cheeks. "Please." Moira the rebel, the one who made others cry, was crying.

He held up her tiny kitten and examined him. "Hurt this little guy?" He turned back to Moira with a frown so big his face almost broke from it. "What do you take me for? I'm not a monster. I'd never hurt a kitten." He dropped the kitten back into his lap and petted it as it purred and purred and purred. "While I was waiting for you, we've become good friends."

I probed his mind. He truly did like kittens. And puppies. And huge, ugly, guard dogs. And Moira. Most of all, he liked Moira. I checked her expression because it was hard for me to realize she couldn't read that attraction. But she couldn't because she was normal. Getting to understand normal people was challenging. I backed up a step and watched them. This could be interesting.

Moira breathed again when she realized her kitten wasn't in immediate danger. But she was still the rebel, the girl who didn't trust anyone and he might have future plans for her small friend. "Then why are you here?" She tensed inside, ready to grab her kitten and disappear the first chance she got if there was any indication of future malice.

The Security guy petted the kitten once more and it purred harder. "I don't know its name, that's why I'm here. I need a name in order to fill in the manifest correctly to make him a legal occupant of Nova One. And age. And sex."

He stared at Moira as if she was a truant, which she'd been enough times growing up to recognize the expression, similar to those of many principals she'd met over the years in their offices where she'd been sent for one infraction or another.

"I tried to make an appointment with a vet to get him examined and have a chip implanted."

Another severe look in Moira's direction. "All pets must have a chip, you know. But I couldn't make the appointment because I don't know its name so couldn't fill in the required information. Or sex, until just now you said it's a boy."

"You're not going to turn him in?" Moira was beginning to relax but was still wary.

He sighed, also like many principals she'd met while attending school – or not attending school when she should have – and said, "Of course not but if you don't answer a few simple questions I'm going to have to work doubly hard to make this little guy officially a part of the Nova One community." He cuddled the kitten a bit more and then looked back at her. "So what's his name?"

"I never got around to naming him. I was busy getting ready to leave Earth. He's not very old, you know."

"So I see." He raised the kitten high and tickled its belly. "Well he needs a name and he needs it now." He scowled. "I should get him registered today because we're just starting and confusion is everywhere but the longer you wait to give this guy a name the harder it'll be." His eyes slitted. "So come up with a name fast or who knows whether this little deception will work."

Moira couldn't think. She was that scared. She

went blank and it was all she could do to maintain her bluster. The kitten was that important to her. I wished I could send a mental signal that this man meant no harm. He truly wanted to help. But I couldn't and it was all she could do to face this person who could make or break her kitten's future. She couldn't possibly come up with a name. She could barely remember her own.

He seemed to understand. He brought the kitten close to his face and examined him. "Ghost?" Moira managed to shake her head. "Kat?" She shook her head again. "What then? It's your kitten, you name him."

I thought about the journey we were on, the miles we'd already traveled and the uncountable miles we still had to go, and I took pity on Moira and said, "Traveler?" She looked at me and nodded dumbly, still unable to speak.

The Security type cocked his head and snuggled the small kitten against his cheek. "Traveler it is, and I can say with some authority that he's not the only cat or dog named Traveler on Nova One. Hundreds of them. Maybe more." He rose and placed Traveler gently on the chair. "Now that I know his name and sex, I can finish making him a legitimate member of the community and make an appointment with a vet."

Then he left. Just like that and it was all Moira could do to walk across the floor and fall into the chair he'd just vacated and let Traveler jump into her lap and purr exactly as he'd done with the Security guard whose name she didn't know who would be back with a time and place for a vet appointment for the tiny kitten whose food she'd not have to steal after all because he'd be legal and everything. She didn't know the guard's name but that was a small thing. He'd saved

Traveler from a terrible fate. Traveler was safe.

Except she was curious about him for more reasons than just one small kitten. He was a hunk and she'd noticed. Hmmmm. What would become of them in the future? I figured I'd probably find out because without anything having been said, it seemed that Moira and I were, indeed, friends.

Moira filled Traveler's food dish and didn't worry how much was left because she could get more simply by walking into a store and getting it. We ate hamburgers as Traveler ate his kitty food but I was pretty sure Moira wouldn't remember any of it. She was still that shook up. When dinner was done, I watched Traveler climb Moira's leg and rest on her shoulder. Then I left the two of them and returned to my own apartment, wondering when and if I'd ever meet the Security guard again.

Turned out the next evening one of us did meet him. Moira. I'd done what would be unforgiveable if I was still on Earth. I'd scraped a small area of my uncle's thought-block from the wall between our apartments because I really did want to make sure Traveler would be safe. If anything seemed wrong I was determined to rush over and help Moira save him.

I opened a can of spaghetti as I read her thoughts about dinner. She hadn't reached the stage of actually making a decision as to what to eat when there was a knock on her door. She opened it and the Security guard walked in as if he belonged. Which he did as far as Traveler was concerned because the small kitten climbed his leg and insisted on riding his shoulder as he strode across the room to where Moira was staring into a pantry that was totally empty.

"Empty. Not very appetizing."

"I haven't gone shopping yet."

He stroked Traveler. "He's registered, he's official, and he has an appointment with a vet two days from now." He looked like he could purr along with Traveler. He was proud of his deception. "He can come and go without being arrested." He took the tiny kitten and placed him on a chair and Traveler promptly curled up and went to sleep. He was that comfortable with his new home and Moira's visitor. That secure. "What say we go someplace and get something to eat since you have nothing beyond cat food?"

So they went looking for a quick meal. I stepped outside of my apartment and brought my can of cold spaghetti to eat while I listened to their thoughts. I'd given up totally on being polite. I wanted to follow this budding friendship. Or romance. Whatever it turned out to be. Something normal and I needed normal.

Just as everyone had been exploring their new home the previous day, practically everyone must have decided to have a quiet evening that day so it was easy for them to find a pizza place with no line and almost immediately they were sitting at an outside table under a tree of unknown species while I found a bench out of sight but close enough to read their minds.

Outside being a relative term because they were outside the pizza place but inside Nova One, so was that outside or inside? I decided there were many things to learn about this new life. Like the tree of unknown species they sat beneath that was similar to the one I was sitting beneath that had probably been designed specifically for Nova One. Lots of leaves, short and stubby and guaranteed to do well on a new planet no matter what that planet was like. They held huge mugs of root beer to go with the pizza and stared at each other and I wished I had a drink to go with my spaghetti but all I'd had in my apartment was water so I had to be content with that.

Moira looked at the Security type through narrowed eyes. "So tell me what's going on." She'd have slammed her mug on the table for emphasis except she didn't want to attract attention but a lifetime of bluffing her way through all kinds of situations had taught her the value of attack. I tucked that information in my mind for future use. Normal people used verbal bluffs the way mind-readers used mental ones.

She wanted answers and was determined to get some. "Why'd you let me bring Traveler on board when it's clearly against regulations and you are Security so it's your job to stop people like me from doing what I did?" Emboldened by the fact that he didn't blink, she asked another question. "Are you some kind of weirdo? A Security guard who doesn't believe in Security? A rebel?"

He leaned back and examined the leaves overhead, wondering himself what kind of tree it was and if it had ever existed on Earth. "No. Not a rebel. Never was and never will be."

"Then why?"

A tremor so slight she'd have missed it if she wasn't watching him closely went through his body, head to toe and back again. Then he set his root beer on the table and let his body go loose, blinked a couple of times in thought, and spoke. "Because at least half the colonists are rebels and if we stopped every one of them from doing whatever it is they do, then there wouldn't be enough people to go where we're going and do what we're going to do."

"Huh?" Moira couldn't take in what he'd said. "That's crazy."

His hand made a lazy motion in the air and he took another drag on his root beer before continuing. "Think about it, Moira." So he knew her name. Of course he did. He probably knew each and every thing she'd done in her entire life.

But he was here now, talking to her, smiling a lazy, knowing smile, liking her more and more every minute, eating pizza, and sipping root beer. "What kind of people volunteer for something like this? Leaving everything for a trip across the stars with no return? No refund if you change your mind? Do timid people choose to come? Those who are content with their lives? Placid people? Or are the volunteers mostly rebels like you?"

"I never thought of it that way." Moira's thoughts said her sister would never have come no matter what she said. Greta loved her home, her life, the day-to-day ordinariness of it.

"Not everyone on board is like you, of course. They aren't all rebels. There are people who want a new start and people who are running from something and just people who had nothing better to look forward to. But at least half could be your clones and we in Security were trained to deal with all kinds of colonists. We spent many months learning about people, including ones like you. Your bad points. Your good points. And we were taught to use our best judgement when situations arise like one with a small, cuddly kitten in a backpack."

"Oh." What else could she say? For the first time in her life, Moira was deflated. Totally.

The guard waved a piece of pizza and changed the topic. As if rebels and kittens in backpacks weren't important and, in a way, they weren't, not anymore. We were all here, we were on our way. The future was important, not what brought us to this point. "So what do you think of Nova One so far?"

He'd been on board for months already preparing for colonists and for Nova One to leave the solar system. Making ready for new people and new places. He was kind of an expert and Moira decided impulsively that she wanted to know this man better because he could teach her more about Nova One and her new life than anyone she'd met so far or any class she'd taken. He took a bite of pizza and closed his eyes in enjoyment. "Do you think you'll like it?"

"Yes, I will. I already do." The stress of the last couple days slid from her body and was replaced by a warm feeling that encompassed one small kitten, one rather large and good-looking security guard, many thousands of colonists, half of whom were just like her, and Nova One itself. I envied her that feeling. Maybe someday I'd feel the same. Maybe.

Moira looked around. Through her mind I saw the table where they sat, the park that was inside and outside at the same time. The lack of money. The fact that rules were rules but bendable in the proper circumstances and I unexpectedly found myself thinking the same thing Moira was thinking. That we'd spend the rest of our lives here if the planet we were headed towards proved not suitable for colonization. In that case Nova One would continue on for generations until the right planet was found. Or forever.

Even if the planet was perfect, neither Moira nor I nor that Security guard would see our new home until we were years older than when our journey began but those years of travel through empty space suddenly didn't matter because the journey had begun and we were part of it. That simple fact was the important thing.

So maybe I'd been looking at the going-into-space-for-all-mankind thing all wrong. Maybe it was an adventure after all and I should just go with the flow. Maybe I'd come to be as enthusiastic as Moira and the Security guard. Maybe. Hopefully.

As those thoughts went through my mind, the Security guard finished his root beer and stood up. Started away. Stopped. Turned back. And spoke. "By the way, my name is Jake. See you around."

As Moira watched him disappear around a building, she wondered what he meant by those words. She almost panicked before reminding herself that Jake really did like kittens. But as for me, I'd heard enough. I rose from my bench, threw my empty spaghetti can into the nearest recycling bin and headed for a store for a six pack of pop.

I knew why Jake had gone to so much trouble to save Moira's kitten. Besides being a kitten lover, of course. He'd mostly done those things because he liked Moira and hoped to get to know her better.

The potential budding romance made me smile for the first time since boarding the complex and highly technological tin can that was Nova One. If one small kitten, one rebellious girl and one Security guard could become friends and have a good life on board this starship, perhaps I could too.

I reached my apartment, went inside, and applied a bit more of my uncle's thought-blocking spray to completely seal off Moira's apartment and her thoughts from my all-too-nosy mind. Because, much as I wanted to follow her relationship with Jake, my parents had instilled some standards of decency and privacy in me after all and spying on someone else's romance wasn't acceptable. Darn.

I opened a can of pop, plopped down on the sofa, turned on that quantum entangled communication system and called my parents to let them know I was well and adjusting to life in Nova One as the huge tin can headed for the vast reaches of space between the stars and sped up imperceptibly towards the speed of light and beyond.

CHAPTER 4

I FALL IN LUST

After searching for intelligent life without success, their makers finally decided there probably weren't any other intelligent beings in the Universe. The thought made them sad, though their creations could not share their sadness because feelings were not programmed into them. Emotion was not a requirement for their mission so wasn't programmed into them in much the same way that they weren't designed to make existential decisions because it wasn't expected there'd be a need for them.

———————— • ● • ————————

I sat in my apartment the next day and considered my life. Not Moira's life. Not the life of her kitten or the Security type who saved him. I considered my life. Mine. Just mine. I decided it was time I actually got a life instead of living second-hand through her. So I approached my coffee table and considered the pamphlets spread across it that were there when I boarded, as in every apartment on Nova One belonging to the younger generation.

In it was an admonition to choose a job and become skilled at it because, as the pamphlet said, a new world would need every skill imaginable so as long as there weren't too many people in whatever field I chose I could do whatever I wished with my life except be lazy. I decided to take the pamphlet to heart and do something. But what?

I leafed through an endless list of fields of study and chose health care because that's what a lot of people in my community chose. Reading minds is a valuable asset when figuring out what's wrong with a sick or injured person. Reading their pain, their thoughts, the memories that lurk at the edges of their minds that they aren't even aware of that can be important.

I decided to start out as a nurse's aide because it was a low-level job that would be easy to back out of if health care didn't turn out to be the right fit and the training wouldn't take too long. Not to mention that nurse's aides aren't noticed and I most definitely didn't want to be noticed.

The classes weren't hard, the hands-on training was somewhat interesting, and the people were nice, which was a surprise. I liked those who were teaching, my fellow students, and the patients the experienced people dealt with while we watched and learned what to do when it was our turn.

For the first time in my life I worked with normal people. I learned to help normal people. I'd not been around normal people much growing up. My community was intentionally isolated. To my complete surprise, I found I actually made friends with some of them which was a good thing because no one else on Nova One was like me and if I wanted friends, normal people were the only option.

When the training ended we were all sent to clinics to begin our actual jobs. I was sent to the clinic on Deck Five because that's where I lived. I reported to a gray-haired, middle-aged nurse named Fiona. Her boss, Dr. Smith, an equally gray-haired middle aged general practitioner, ran the clinic. But there was also a second doctor.

Dr. Riley Nugent was young, probably just out of medical school. He was tallish and had dark brown hair and eyes and a permanent tan that said he might be multi-racial and he was gorgeous and every female in the clinic, myself included, fell instantly in lust with him because, miracle of miracles, he was not only every woman's fantasy, he was single.

Of course he didn't notice a lowly aide like me.

Until he did.

One day about a week after starting my job as a nurse's aide, I was talking with a patient, a little boy of about five named Nate who'd been knocked unconscious when he fell from a slide and hit his head. His mother said he liked baseball so I talked with him about that to see if he was rational. And I listened to his thoughts to determine if he was thinking straight. Of course, no one else knew I read his mind.

As Nate talked his thoughts gradually grew fuzzier and fuzzier. I was about to ask another question when I felt a prickling along my spine that alerted me that someone was watching me. Not Nate's mother. Someone else.

Who was it and why were they watching? I knew whoever it was hadn't been watching until I started caring for Nate. So was I the focus of attention or was Nate? I sent out mental feelers as I'd been taught as a kid and searched through the room.

I found nothing and I'm normally exceptionally good at reading minds. I always excelled in school. I should have easily located the watcher and read his or her thoughts so a prickle of fear coursed through me. What was wrong? Was I losing my powers?

I turned as casually as possible and checked out the room and found myself looking squarely into Dr. Nugent's eyes. He was the watcher, no doubt about it, and his eyebrows were drawn together in thought. But I couldn't read his mind. That, more than his penetrating gaze, scared the crap out of me. I'd never before failed to read the mind of a person who wasn't blocking their thoughts.

I panicked. I took deep breaths and tried to talk myself out of another panic attack. Then I looked towards him again, surreptitiously this time, but all I learned from that look was that his eyes were the color of molasses and as deeply beautiful as the stars. His mind was still closed off from me.

I'd never learned to read faces because I could read thoughts and that had been enough. Now it wasn't. Now I wished I could read Dr. Nugent's expression. Then Nate's thoughts cut into my panic because they were growing more and more cloudy. He was going downhill fast. I snapped back to my job and read Nate's thoughts – or lack of them -- and took a deep breath and turned to the nurse, Fiona, and mouthed, "He's not right."

"He looks fine to me." She sounded a bit annoyed.

"He's not as well as he appears."

"What makes you think so?"

What could I say? That I knew his thoughts weren't coherent because I'd read his mind? "It's just – just –"

"He's fine," She prepared to send him home. But he shouldn't go. He needed to be monitored.

Nurse Fiona reached for Nate. I reached for him at the same time. Her lips tightened. *'Brand new nurse's aide thinks she knows more than we professionals.'*

I pulled back, and then tried and failed to come up with a reason to retain the small child and surrendered little Nate, knowing he wasn't well but not knowing what else I could do.

"I think we'll keep him for a while." Nurse Fiona and I both looked up as Dr. Nugent came smoothly between us and knelt before Nate. "How are you doing, big guy?" Nate looked at this new person blankly because his thoughts were growing more cloudy with each passing moment. "Want to stick around a bit? Your mom can stay too." He smiled at Nate's mother who stood to one side.

Nurse Fiona's eyes slitted. Dr. Nugent was paying more attention to the ramblings of a mere aide than to the professional opinion of a nurse and she didn't like it. *'She's young and cute and has him forgetting he's a doctor.'* She pretended to examine Nate but her thoughts were about me. *'I'll deal with her later. She'll learn how things are done around here. Whose word counts.'*

Dr. Nugent took Nate by the elbow and helped him stand, preparatory to taking him to one of the rooms that lined the hall. Before he took a single step, Nate puked. Swayed. Would have fallen if not for Dr. Nugent's hands on his little body.

Nate's breakfast splattered all over the hall floor. Nurse Fiona's thoughts changed instantaneously to professional mode as she and the doctor brought Nate to a bed. She forgot all about me in her concern for her small patient.

She was a good nurse. She cared about her patients. She just didn't like uppity aides and in the last few minutes she'd decided that she definitely didn't like me. But I hoped the confusion would make her forget I existed.

Didn't happen. When she returned a while later, after Nate was stable and Dr. Nugent had left for his next patient, she saw me and remembered. *'How'd she know Nate was sicker than he appeared? Was it a lucky guess?'* As she stared at me in the corridor, she decided that must have been what happened and turned away as another patient appeared. But in her mind I'd become a problem to be dealt with. *'I'll take care of her.'*

Her antagonism haunted me. Had I made a mistake in choosing health care? If I was found out, what would happen? I was on a starship, I couldn't just quit and go home to my safe, isolated community. I spent a sleepless night and was red-eyed and tired when I returned to the clinic the next morning.

That day passed without incident but all day I felt Dr. Nugent watching me, assessing me, even as Nurse Fiona watched his interest and thought how best to put me in my place. *'I'll take care of her.'*

Nurse Fiona's mind was loud and nasty. Why couldn't I read Dr. Nugent's mind?

That night I contacted my parents via the quantum entangled communication system that would keep us in contact with one another until we entered hyperspace and asked if anyone in the community had ever failed to read someone's mind.

"It happens now and then," was all my dad said and I actually howled at learning such an important thing after I was an adult and trillions of miles from home.

"It's more common than you'd think," my mom added, her voice only slightly guilty at their lack of parental guidance. "I can't read your father's mind and he can't read mine. We figure it's for the best because too much closeness isn't good for any couple." Then she added, "Sorry for not mentioning it."

My father chimed in. "It's usually an emotional thing. It happens between people with a deep emotional attachment."

"That's not what's happening here, I hardly know Dr. Nugent," I replied, glad the mind-reading thing didn't work long distance so they couldn't know that they'd just explained why I couldn't read the sexy doctor's mind. Because there was a whole lot of emotion in our relationship even though it was all on my side. It was evidently enough to blank out the mind-reading thing. Darn.

I told them the other thing that bothered me about Dr. Nugent. "I don't know why he keeps watching me. It's scary."

"He's normal, remember. You're not used to normal people. You're probably reading too much into his way of making sure you give his patients good care."

Mom agreed. "He sounds like a nice man."

No help from my parents on that front. But it calmed me somewhat to know that not everyone's mind can be read. That night I slept.

The next day a middle-aged man came to the clinic. He was pallid and shaking and generally in a bad way. The opinion of those with medical degrees was that he was experiencing a panic attack brought on by the realization that he'd never return to Earth. I heard them telling each other this wasn't the first such case.

Except he wasn't having a panic attack. He was truly ill. He was struggling to handle his pain and trying to push it away by thinking about the trip we were on but he couldn't and so panic was setting in because he'd come for help only to learn that no one believed him. And the only symptom the professionals saw was that panic. Not the pain.

Soon he actually would be in full panic mode caused by his fear of being ignored and that panic might disguise his very real physical ailment. He needed help and I knew it. But I was a brand-new aide and Nurse Fiona was determined to put me in my place so there wasn't anything I could do. Actually, no one in the entire clinic would pay attention to the ramblings of a lowly aide. Why would they? I was the lowest of the low.

Except Dr. Nugent. He turned to me. "What do you think?"

I bit my lower lip as Nurse Fiona glowered. But I spoke honestly. "He's in pain. It's real pain. It's not imaginary."

He blinked slowly, his expression blank. "How do you know?"

Nurse Fiona stared at me with hate. *"There she goes again. She thinks she's so smart. She needs to be taken down a peg and I'm the one to do it.'*

I curled into myself but I didn't keep quiet. "I just know."

Dr. Nugent thought a moment and then turned to the patient. "Show me where it hurts."

The man touched his lower stomach. "Here."

Dr. Nugent frowned. "Appendicitis?" He told the patient to straighten his legs and he did.

Nurse Fiona smiled in triumph and gave me a look of pure poison. "Not appendicitis if he can straighten his legs."

"You'd think so." Dr. Nuget's head tilted and he met my look with a piercing question and I wanted to tell him how I knew about the pain but I couldn't. Just that it was real. Our looks held as those nut-brown eyes tried to know what I knew and he finally said, "Not everyone has classic symptoms." He smiled encouragingly at the patient. "We'll run a few tests."

The rising panic the patient had been experiencing disappeared. Someone was listening to him. He wasn't being ignored. He'd be tested and treated. He slumped in relief. Nurse Fiona noticed. "See. He just relaxed. He's not in real pain and I knew it."

"A few tests won't hurt and then we'll know," Dr. Nugent said soothingly, and I wondered if he'd had problems with Nurse Fiona before.

A few hours later, the patient's infected appendix was gone, he was sleeping peacefully, and Nurse Fiona was seething with anger because, in her mind, I'd intentionally made her look bad.

Dr. Nugent measured her anger, which told me that

he had, indeed, had to deal with her before. He nodded to me. "It's quiet now so what say you go for lunch even though it's a bit early?" He stretched as if something had just occurred to him. "In fact, I think I'll do the same."

He peered at the time pretending to just now realize how late it was. "It's getting time that I can call it a day because Dr. Smith will be here in less than an hour. There's no need for me to stick around until then." He turned to Nurse Fiona. "You can handle things." He smiled broadly at her. "I trust your professional competence."

She assured him that she could, indeed, handle anything and I left, shooed out by Dr. Nugent who followed close behind, shaking his head and rolling his eyes while not giving me a chance to say a word before shepherding me towards the hole-in-the-wall café near the clinic where we unimportant types often had lunch while the doctors normally went elsewhere. Then he simply said, "I hope you like hot dogs because I happen to be a hot dog afficiando and I want to talk with you." As we went inside, he added, "Because I've been watching you."

If I'd had anything in my stomach, I'd have puked.

CHAPTER 5

I TELL RILEY THE TRUTH

Their creations did not remain as they were made. As they found new things in the vastness of space they learned and grew in every way imaginable. They became more than when they were made. More aware. More curious. More sentient. Over time they became fully functional, thinking beings. Their makers approved because higher level thinking gave them more ability to deal with situations they encountered in their travels through the Universe.

So they continued on as they were programmed to do, wandering the Universe and reporting back on a regular schedule.

— • ● • —

Dr. Nugent ordered hot dogs for both of us but I played with mine, not eating because I didn't know if it would stay down. How can a criminal eat a last meal? I couldn't and that was how I saw that hot dog. As my last meal before being condemned as a pervert.

"So, tell me about this gift you have," Dr. Nugent said in a voice so gentle that I knew it was fake. Had to be. He was normal, after all, and that meant he shouldn't be trusted.

"Uh – Dr. Nugent – uh –" I spilled mustard on the table. He handed me a napkin and I fussed with it to give myself time to think.

"My name's Riley. When we're not at work. When we're eating hot dogs."

"Riley –"

He sighed and looked at me in much the way he'd looked at little Nate. Like a problem to be solved. "I've noticed how you connect with our patients. To people in general, I believe." He smiled encouragingly. "Lots of people are sympathetic. Empathic. It helps in medicine." He leaned back and examined me from a different perspective. "In fact I believe you are the most empathic person I've ever seen." He tapped his cheek and tried to put me at ease and failed because I couldn't relax.

He leaned closer until I could smell the minty, medicinal soap the clinic provided. "I don't mean to pry, it's not that. This isn't an inquest. If your unusually keen empathy is the result of a difficult childhood, well then I don't mean to make you relive trauma even if it happened long ago."

His brow furrowed and he touched my hand on the table lightly. Then he took another napkin and wiped a bit of mustard off my chin that had dripped on me during the mustard episode. But he said nothing. He just waited.

The thing was, I didn't have a difficult childhood,

as he believed, and I didn't want him to think badly of my parents. The worst thing they'd ever done was not mention that I might not be able to read the mind of someone I was emotionally attached to. Like Dr. Nugent. Riley.

"My parents are nice. My childhood was happy."

"Good to know." Silence grew between us as he continued to examine me. "So how is it that you understand people so well? Are you some kind of mind reader?"

I'd started on my hot dog. I'd taken a single, exploratory bite to see how it would sit in my stomach because maybe I could eat lunch after all. I was hungry, having skipped breakfast. But his words made me choke on my hot dog and turn away so he couldn't see my face. I literally gagged.

He rose, came around, examined me with professional precision, and decided I wasn't about to choke to death in the next few seconds. So he returned to his chair and waited for me to come back to the real world.

The normal world. The world I would spend the rest of my life living in and that thought shook me as nothing had done since arriving on Nova One and caused a panic attack like the ones of the people who had come on board and lived happily until something suddenly made them realize they were in space and headed away from Earth and safety as fast as Nova One could go. I suddenly realized I'd never be safe again.

Dr. Nugent -- Riley – recognized what was happening. He expertly took the hot dog from my clutching hand, pulled me upright, and then wrapped one arm around my shoulders and steered me out of the hot dog place so skillfully that no one even noticed that a madwoman was having a meltdown next to the pop machine.

"Where do you live?" was all he asked as he half carried, half dragged me towards the nearest housing complex which wasn't far because it was most efficient for people to live near where they worked in case of disaster. Shorter distance to run in a ship-wide emergency.

I pointed to my hallway and soon we were in my apartment, me curled in the fetal position on the couch and Dr. Nugent – Riley – beside me with an arm around me in case I fell. Or to keep me safe. What he unknowingly was doing was sending me into paroxysms of lust.

It was the lust thing that brought me out of my panic attack because it was impossible to panic decently while sitting thigh to thigh with the man all female medical types swooned over.

"Sorry I caused this," he said soothingly as he checked me competently for signs of further trauma. Finding none, he backed away, which allowed me to breathe. Then, curious, he asked cautiously, "Am I that scary or did you just now realize you're leaving Earth and so succumbed to the panic attack that's so common lately?"

I'd opened my mouth to reply with no idea what I'd say when my parents called. Seems my little cousin was visiting and was curious about Nova One so they decided to let him ask me questions directly. My cousin sat between them at the table, sticking out his tongue at me and giggling.

That's what I saw on my screen. What they saw

was me shaking in terror and curled up on the couch with a doctor, complete with white medical jacket, examining me. "What's wrong?" my dad asked as he practically crawled through quantum space to get to his daughter and help. Because that's what dads do.

"She's okay now," Riley said in his best soothing doctor voice, the same one I'd heard him use with numerous distraught family members. "She was upset, that's all." He shrugged while thinking how to pacify family members long distance. "It happens. I was around so I brought her home." Because he was clearly a doctor but he wanted them to know this wasn't a medical emergency. "She's fine. You don't have to worry."

"Who are you?" My dad used his best protect-his-daughter voice.

"Dr. Nugent. Riley. We work at the same clinic." He examined the family around the kitchen table and decided to elaborate because they clearly needed more information. "We were having lunch when she had a slight problem with a hot dog." He cleared his throat as people do when covering a lie "I insisted she come home and I came along to make sure she's okay." He put on his most professional smile. "Which she is."

"Dr. Nugent?" My mom stared at him. "She's mentioned you." Seeing my horrified reaction to her statement, she added, "Along with her other co-workers."

My dad wasn't convinced I was okay. "A hot dog? Never. Not my Anna." The hot dog lover of the world, he could have added.

Dr. Nugent examined him and decided it would be best to say more. "Actually, I might have said something to upset her."

"You? What did you say?" Fatherly protection was in every word.

Riley ran his fingers through his hair. "To be honest, I'm not sure. I've noticed that Anna is quite good with patients. She sympathizes with them to an extraordinary degree. She's quite empathic. I was mentioning that when something upset her." His hands went out. "I'm sorry. I didn't mean to say the wrong thing."

My parents instantly knew what had happened, that I'd panicked at the possibility of my secret being compromised. My cousin, on the other hand, was barely in school and had just recently learned that we were 'different' and had also just recently been told that it shouldn't be discussed. Like all of us at his age, he'd been told to keep quiet about our special powers. But he wanted to brag instead.

He spoke up. "Of course, she got upset because she's different than you – we're all different -- and you sure did say the wrong thing." He snickered. "It wouldn't have bothered me because I'm not scared of anything."

My parents stared at my cousin, trying to silence him, but he kept talking. "We're never supposed to tell people about us." He waved at the quantum communication screen. "But why not? It's a stupid rule."

Riley turned to me. His eyes narrowed as he saw that my breathing had stopped the instant my parents tried to silence my cousin. But he said nothing, turning back to my family and saying in a very quiet voice, "What do you know about Anna that I don't know but should?" When they remained silent, he added, "Because, from your behavior now and the way Anna panicked, I suspect something is going on. In fact I know so and that it's important." He waited and when they said nothing, he repeated. "Possibly very important."

My father sighed. He gave my cousin a look that said he'd deal with him later and then he looked at me with another look that said he hoped he was doing the right thing and said, "Anna is special. You've recognized her specialness and you're right, she has a gift. The thing is, we don't want anything to happen to her because of it. So we don't mention it." His eyes narrowed and if he'd been close, he'd have nailed Riley to the wall for emphasis. "But the only thing you need to know about her specialness right now, Dr. Nugent, is that you'd better think hard about possible consequences if anything happens to her."

Riley's brows knitted. This wasn't the answer he'd been looking for. "I agree that she has a gift. That's evident in her work. I just don't understand what it is. How it works." He examined my family around the kitchen table all those millions of miles away. "Perhaps you can explain."

My parents looked at one another and my father shook his head before turning back to Riley. "If Anna wants you to know, she'll tell you." He reached for the switch to end the conversation, but before flipping it, he added, "For now it's enough for you to know that you'd best not mess with my little girl. She's not the only one in the family with a gift."

Then the screen went dark. Riley stared for a long time at the blank wall. "What was that all about?" And then added, "Tell me." Remembering my dad's words, he added, "If you choose to do so."

What to say? What lie would make him stop asking questions?

His eyes held me. His voice, soft and reassuring, said he'd never harm me. But he didn't know me, not really.

We stared at one another almost without blinking as I thought what to say. So far no one on Nova One knew the truth about me. That kept me safe. If I told someone, even one person, even someone I trusted, and the truth got out, I could be in danger.

I took a deep breath. Stared at him. And spoke. "I can read minds."

I didn't mean to say it. I knew a hundred lies, many hundreds of excuses I'd been taught in school to use if I was confronted by suspicious people but that day I didn't use any of them. I told him the truth.

He folded his arms and considered me. Not as a madwoman or an idiot or a liar. Just looked at me. "Prove it." His arms unfolded. "Tell me what I'm thinking."

"I can't." He'd not believe me. Of course he wouldn't believe I could read minds if I couldn't read his. "For some reason I don't understand I can't read your mind." Should I be glad he'd never know the real reason? The in-lust-with-him thing?

He chewed his lower lip. "Okay. You can't read my mind but you say you can read the thoughts of other people. Let's go somewhere. Find some people. Then you read their minds." Remembering my father's admonition, he added, "If you want me to believe you. If not, we'll forget this very strange conversation ever happened."

I rose and for some reason felt almost good. Right. I'd been keeping a huge secret and the secrecy had harmed me. Secrets were hard, I decided, too hard for me. I needed someone else to know what I could do.

Besides, I wanted to share myself and my gift with another human being just as I'd shared with my family growing up. Riley was the logical choice. The only choice it seemed.

I led us from my apartment back to that hot dog place because it had been early when we were there before but now lunch would be in full swing so there'd be lots of people. Riley followed without a word, without touching me.

We got pop as an excuse for being there but not food because neither of us felt like eating. And I looked around and opened my mind to the cacophony of thoughts bouncing around the room. Then I looked at Riley. "There." I pointed to a mother with a small child. "Her daughter wants cherry pop but the mother wants her to have milk instead. They are going to argue."

Riley's eyebrows rose but he watched the pair across the room. The mother reached for a carton of milk from the refrigerator. The daughter tugged at her mother's shirt. "No milk. I want pop." She pointed to the pop case. "I want red pop."

Riley's eyes widened. His hands went still, his own pop that was half-way to his mouth stopped in mid-air. Noticing, he made himself take a swig before setting it carefully in the exact center of the table. "Could have been a coincidence. All kids want pop and red catches their attention. I'd have said the same thing when I was a kid."

I looked around some more. A middle-aged man was about to give his order. "He'll want two hot dogs with chili and will ask if they have extra-spicy condiments because if he can't get them the way he wants, he'll leave."

Riley rose and dragged me after him as we went closer to hear the man talk. "Two dogs, with chili and where do you keep the hot stuff? The spicy stuff?" The girl behind the counter said everything they had was on the condiment table and the man sniffed and cancelled his order. He turned smartly and left. The girl behind the counter watched him go and rolled her eyes and waited on the next customer.

"You got that right." He pulled me to a comparatively quiet corner. "It wasn't the kind of thing you could guess. It was specific. And right. So maybe you can do what you say. Maybe."

"Shhhh!" I looked around in panic to see if anyone had heard but no one was paying attention to us. "Don't say anything out loud. It's dangerous! Please!"

He kind of shook his head as if wondering whether he was in an alternate reality. Then he grabbed me by the hand once more and led me out of there as quickly as possible and we didn't stop until we were in another apartment in the same complex as mine but this one was his.

It was identical to mine in every respect except for personal touches because Nova One didn't distinguish between higher-ups like doctors and lowly peons like me. Everyone got the same living arrangement that was based on the number of people in a household. They also got the same food, the same everything. Except recognition. The thing that separated the important people from people like me was that everyone knew who was important.

Riley was a doctor and garnered attention everywhere he went because he was a good doctor and word got around. His apartment, though, was lacking anything that spoke of a personal style. It was exactly as when he'd moved in. The man must live for his work. Or didn't know how to decorate.

"Tell me about this mind reading thing. How it works. Why you can do it. How often. Anything and everything." He fought the impulse to make it an order. As a doctor he was used to giving orders. But my dad had made an impression. "If you want to tell me, that is."

I said nothing. He rubbed the back of his neck. Stared at me. Shot a look towards the ceiling. Then, as suddenly as the sun coming out after a squall, something occurred to him and he changed. Smiled. Grinned. Chuckled. "Tell me everything I need to know to protect you from Nurse Fiona."

I giggled. What else could I do with him looking so sexy and laughing about Nurse Fiona? So I told him, hesitantly at first and then with the words pouring out. What it was like growing up in an isolated community. Learning I was different. Wanting to read minds and not wanting to because it meant I was different. Learning that it was our responsibility to use our gifts even if we got punished for it. Applying for Nova One. Being accepted. Deciding to go into medicine and becoming an aide because it didn't require extensive education.

I spread my hands. "So that's it."

"Your ability helps people."

"It's dangerous if people figure it out."

"You're talking about Nurse Fiona."

"She's only the first. Other's will notice eventually."

He blinked, then said, "I'll protect you."

"You can't."

"I'll handle Nurse Fiona. We'll deal with others as needed."

"You can't, not without exposing me. What will you tell her next time she thinks I'm showing her up?"

"I don't know." He raked one hand through his hair. "I just know that I'll keep your secret and keep you safe." He lowered his hand and took one of mine. "I won't let your ability put you in danger because your people are right, it can help humanity." Then, remembering my dad's threat, he asked with a grimace, "What other powers do you people possess? What can your father do that can reach through space and destroy me if anything bad happens to you?"

"It's just Dad power. Nothing more."

"A bluff?"

"Yep."

"It worked." Riley looked relieved. But he wasn't finished. "Medicine is good but considering nurse Fiona and others like her, I believe it could be dangerous. So maybe it would be best to switch to something different."

"Such as?"

"I don't know but I'll help you figure it out if you agree that medicine isn't right for you." He took both of my hands in his. "Did you know that the moment I laid eyes on you somehow I knew you were special? I just didn't know in what way. But I know now and I'll keep you safe because your father's too far away to handle the job."

"I can take care of myself." Irritation flowed through me. Did he see me as an infant? A child? An incompetent adult? No way! "I don't need any help."

"From what you've just told me, yes you do. Your life has been isolated. You need protection until you get used to the normal world." I couldn't argue with his logic and at some level was glad protecting me meant he'd be in my life. Close. "But until we figure out where to go from here, it'll be best if you continue working at the clinic where I can watch out for you."

"What about Nurse Fiona?" The bane of my existence. "Until I change careers, that is, and yes, you are right, medicine isn't for me."

He raked his fingers through his hair again, a gesture I'd already come to associate with him. "Nurse Fiona." He shuddered and tried to smile but it was lopsided. "I'll see to it that you only work when I'm on duty."

He snapped his fingers to turn on the wall screen. "But since medicine isn't for you, let's find out what else is out there." We ordered takeout and spent the evening scrolling through literally hundreds and hundreds of possible careers, all of which we eliminated.

When I left late that evening, I didn't have a clue what I'd do with my life beyond that I wanted Riley to be a part of it, not because I needed a guardian but because he made my toes curl.

CHAPTER 6

I BECOME A FIRST CONTACT PROFESSIONAL

With each addition of knowledge, their makers marveled at the complexity and beauty of the universe. Each time their creators downloaded copies of their minds and added that knowledge to the data bases they were compiling, their creations knew they had done well and had done what they'd been created to do. If they were capable of feeling emotions they would have been proud. But they weren't because emotion wasn't needed for their jobs so hadn't been programmed into them.

———————•●•———————

The next few days were as uneventful as possible considering I worked in a medical clinic. Riley – Dr. Nugent when we were in the clinic – made good on his promise to be there whenever Nurse Fiona and I were both there and he also, as promised, stuck close enough that nothing untoward happened.

Of course Nurse Fiona noticed. Sniffed whenever she passed me. Sent looks from Riley to me and back again with uplifted eyebrows and clear disgust. '*Little snit. She's after Dr. Nugent. She's using him, of course. Just wants to be seen with a doctor.*' Then, later, '*I'll take care of her. Some day when Dr. Nugent isn't here and following her around like a besotted, love-sick calf.*'

Besotted? Love-sick? Not even close though I wished I could read his mind in case there was even a scrap of feelings for me.

Whenever we met outside of working hours we met at either his place or mine so as to keep our relationship low-key. Since we were practically neighbors that wasn't hard and I soon learned to keep hot dogs in my refrigerator because he truly did like them as much as I did. He liked them every way possible, from chili dripping from a bun to accompanying a pot of beans to every other way I knew and a few I learned from him.

While I learned about hot dogs from an expert, we both learned how many jobs potential colonists could become competent in. The list was overwhelming. One evening, as we scanned the list of jobs colonists must be familiar with and a few no one had ever had reason to learn on Earth, a smile slid across his lips and then slowly, inch by inch, reached his eyes and he relaxed, starting with those deep, brown eyes and flowing down his body until his feet took him to the couch. He pulled me along and plopped me beside him. "First Contact. That's it. The perfect job for you."

He would have turned me towards him except I was already facing him. "Who'd have guessed there are actually classes for people who want to learn to communicate with aliens should we encounter any on our journey? It's a job made for a mind reader because goodness knows they won't speak English."

"No." I explained. "The classes will do it. Someone will figure out about me. I'll be outed."

He considered me. "We can have the lessons come to my apartment. No one need know a thing beyond your name on a list of students. No one will see you in action." He leaned close enough that I could feel his breath. "Of course, it'll mean a lot of time at my place. Are you okay with that?"

Was it? We'd be physically close. Too close considering how I felt. I'd self-incinerate. I should forget the whole thing. I didn't. Instead I asked, "When do we start?" as I headed for the door. "It doesn't matter to me one way or another where I study." I tried to look casual to match my words and failed completely.

He reached the door ahead of me, blocking my way with a hurt expression. "Hey, Anna. If you don't want me around, that's fine. I'm a big boy and can handle a little rejection. You're more than capable of figuring out your own future. I apologize for intruding. It's your call and you're free to live your life however you wish. With or without me."

I wilted. I felt stupid. "Sorry." I thought about the future and compared it to my childhood. How my community's beliefs back on Earth must have gotten to me more than I realized because even here in empty space I believed I had an obligation to humanity. "I'll appreciate all the help you can give."

When we met the next day I told him I'd figured

how to publicly end my career as a nurses' aide without arousing suspicions as to why an aide would quit so soon after starting. "I'm going to inform everyone that I can't handle the sight of blood. Then I'll leave. Immediately."

Riley thought it might work so the next day I told everyone at the clinic my made-up excuse and Nurse Fiona almost crowed. *'About time she came to her senses. Stupid little aide. A couple of good guesses can't substitute for real knowledge.'* Then she gave me a triumphant smile and everyone else gave me a goodbye hug and the next day I started my new classes.

The class was huge which was good because I was lost in the crowd. Evidently a lot of people on Nova One hoped we'd encounter aliens and soon I was well on my way to becoming a First Contact specialist. There was such a thing. It was a genuine course of study.

My teachers said I was a natural, which was true though I never explained why I was so good. Since alien contact might not involve language at all we explored other ways of communicating and I excelled. Of course I did. I had to tamp down on my ability in order to not be noticed too much.

We students spent a lot of time with experts of one kind or another as we became a trained, cohesive, First Contact unit ready to spring into action should we accidentally run across any aliens in the space between the stars. We laughed about the possibility and said it would never happen but no one dropped out. And, though the classes came to Riley's apartment, I ended up spending a lot of time with the other students.

We all spent a fair amount of time on the Bridge

because that was where First Contact would take place if aliens were ever encountered and we had to be comfortable being there and know how things worked.

Eventually I finished my coursework and internship and officially became a First Contact specialist. Riley suggested we celebrate. "Hot dogs?"

"Of course."

We went inside the hot dog hangout and looked around. "Where can we sit?" Because all the tables were occupied.

"We get some hot dogs to go. Then should we celebrate at your place or mine?" I didn't care where we went. I was just glad to be done with classes and be with Riley.

We went to my apartment because it was a kind of family celebration. At Riley's suggestion, we called my family so they could join in. I had pop and ice cream in my refrigerator, something Riley never had because he always ate out. I figured it was a doctor thing.

My parents congratulated me. My father and Riley took each other's measure. Riley whispered, "I'm being vetted. Your father doesn't think I'm good enough for his daughter."

"He'd never think that." But they watched each other the whole time and Riley visibly relaxed when the call was over and my family had told me about a hundred times how proud they were of me, that First Contact sounded interesting and must only be available on starships.

When the call ended, we sat in companionable silence for what seemed like hours and probably was longer. It was beyond late, past the middle of a Nova One fake night.

And still we sat. Silently. Each thinking our own thoughts. Mine were of how odd it was to be comfortable with the doctor I'd once thought of as being so high above lowly aides like me. And of how right it felt at that moment to sit together and do absolutely nothing.

Then Riley said, "This trip is potentially a multi-generational thing if the planet we're headed for isn't suitable."

I yawned. I was that loose. I felt like limp spaghetti and comfortable and strangely happy, something I'd never expected to feel after leaving Earth forever. "So we were told when we signed up."

"What I'm saying is that you might not see those aliens you are so well prepared to communicate with."

"That's a possibility." That would be fine with me.

"There probably won't be aliens in the space between the stars. It'll be more likely when we arrive at whatever planet supports life."

"Yep. Could happen."

"Someone who can read minds should be available when Nova One makes planetfall."

I finally figured out where he was going with that comment. "If not me because the trip can potentially take forever then my child or grandchild. Because mind-reading is inherited."

"Will your children inherit your ability even if the father can't read minds? Because as far as I know you're the only mind-reader on Nova One so the father will be a normal male."

"It's a fairly dominant gene." I stretched because the day had been exciting and now everything was unwinding, including me. Most of all, me. "So there will be more mind-readers even though their father won't be one." I paused. "If I have children."

"You should. For the good of the colony. At least one child. Probably two or three for redundancy."

I giggled. Then I giggled again. "Good plan. Glad you suggested it. Find a willing male and procreate."

"That's the usual route."

"I'll start looking. One of these days."

"I'm volunteering for the job."

"What?" The giggles stopped and the laziness disappeared, replaced by a crisp, clean, jolt of heat that shot straight to the most vulnerable part of my body. "Would you repeat that last sentence?" He did so and I asked, "What exactly are you volunteering for?"

"Helping you to procreate. Last I heard, it takes two and I think we'll make a good couple." A look slid from the corners of his eyes towards me. Judging my response. Wondering if he'd gone too far.

For the thousandth time I wished I could read his mind. But I couldn't because he sent my emotions into overdrive. The emotions I'd once thought were lust. Okay, they were lust but over the months of classes I'd realized that was just part of what I felt.

"I'm stunned." The only words I could think clearly enough to say. He was volunteering to father my children and that involved sex. Wow. That hot blade twisted until my insides were an emotional disaster.

"I'm the only person who knows your secret. That should count for something." He moved closer and that closeness, along with what he'd said and the heat that was now turning my body into pure flame, just about knocked me on my keister. "Should maybe give me an edge on any rivals for your affections."

How many boyfriends did he think I had? Dozens? "No rivals."

"Good to know." A long pause. "So what do you think? Want to make a few mind-reading descendants?"

Was he kidding?! Of course I did and I finally managed to talk enough to let him know that and he didn't leave at all that night and pretty soon everyone in the clinic knew we were an item and everyone was happy for us. Except Nurse Fiona, of course.

"Marry me," Riley said much, much later, when we were almost used to one another.

I didn't expect to say what I said next. Told myself I was insane because any rational, lust-driven woman would want to marry him. But as the words came out, I knew they were right for me. "I'm not ready."

He rubbed his cheek against mine in an unconscious gesture. "Because of the mind-reading thing? Or because of me?'

I pulled him close to me. "It's not you. Never you." I took a deep breath. "I love you." There. I'd said it.

"Me too. I love you." A slight tremor went through his body. "But you're still not ready?'

"Not yet."

All he did was nod that he accepted my decision. "When you're ready, let me know." And we left it at that. Because marriage is hard, and I wanted to wait until I could do it right.

CHAPTER 7

I AM ALMOST MURDERED

As per their original programming, when they returned to their home planet on a regular schedule to report back what they'd learned, they always provided much of interest though they never found intelligent life. Their creators began to think there were no other intelligent beings in the universe and they agreed their makers might be the only intelligent beings anywhere.

———————•●•———————

Riley said not to worry about Nurse Fiona. "What can she do? Nothing because you can read her mind and, anyway, on the rare occasion you might come to the clinic I'll be there."

Time passed and it seemed that he was night. Nothing happened and I only saw her on those times when I met Riley as he was going off duty. I relaxed.

I shouldn't have.

One afternoon I'd arranged to meet Riley at the end

of his shift but he was delayed by a patient with heart problems and he wanted to stay until he was sure the patient was stabilized. So I found a chair in the waiting room, picked up one of the boring magazines Nova One thought we should have that was as much a galactic travel brochure as a real magazine, and started to read.

But getting his patient comfortable took longer than expected and the magazine was really bad. I got antsy and decided to take a stroll through the clinic and see if any of the people I used to work with were still around. I'd say 'hello' and maybe we'd renew a friendship or two. They'd fallen by the wayside when I left because I hadn't realized that relationships with people who couldn't read minds required effort. Connecting mentally is so much easier.

I went looking for Lisa. We'd met while learning how to be aides. I'd heard she'd taken over my spot when I resigned from medicine. It would be nice to have her as a friend again. So I asked if anyone knew where she was and someone pointed to a hallway. "I think I saw her go that way."

I meandered along a seldom used hallway and peeked into what turned out to be an empty room. As I prepared to leave, I heard a sound. Someone was behind me. I sent out mental feelers. And froze because Nurse Fiona stood in the doorway, blocking my way. *'You no longer work here. Did you come to find Dr. Nugent? To bind him even closer to you?'* Out loud, she asked, "What are you doing here?"

"Looking for Lisa."

"She's not here." *'Any excuse to get inside the clinic. It's not enough that she has her talons into him outside of work, now she's hunting him down here.'*

"Guess I'll leave." I tried to get past her and failed.

"Wait." *'We're alone. No one will know and Dr. Nugent will be better off without her.'* Out loud she said in a sticky-sweet voice, "I'd like your help if you have a moment."

Not what I'd expected but she couldn't do anything with all kinds of people close by. Like Riley said, I could scream. She indicated the bed with a set of folded sheets and a pillow in the middle. "Got time to help make it up? There's a patient waiting."

It was a reasonable request. I reached for the sheets. Then I read her thoughts and tried to run but it was too late. She grabbed me and threw me on the bed. *'I have her now. They'll think she just stopped breathing.'*

With what seemed like inhuman strength, she shoved me back onto the bed and pressed the pillow onto my face. I couldn't speak. I couldn't scream for help. I couldn't breathe.

I struggled. I fought. I kicked but she dodged my kick and pressed the pillow more firmly over my face. *'Just a few moments more. She'll stop breathing.'*

I didn't want to die. The thought blasted through my mind as blackness approached. I would not die. Could not die. I had too much to live for. Riley. Nova One. My descendants on some distant planet. First Contact. None would happen if Nurse Fiona succeeded.

The blackness grew. It threatened to envelop me completely.

Then something happened.

My mind met Nurse Fiona's with the brute force of pure desperation. I could feel something starting that was strange and at the same time familiar. Something like reading minds but more. Much more and organically different. I found myself thinking, *'Take away the pillow.'*

I somehow reached straight into her mind and as I fought for life, an impossible thing happened.

She made my thoughts her own. She forgot she'd been trying to kill me. Forgot she hated me. *'This little girl who is helping me make up a bed somehow got a pillow over her head. She can't breathe. How did that happen? I must take away the pillow.'*

The pillow came off. I gulped air as I found myself staring at a changed Nurse Fiona. A different person. I rose, shaking, not knowing what was happening other than that for some unknown reason, she was filled with concern for me. "Are you okay, Anne? You look a bit peaked. You must have fallen and the pillow fell on top of you." She cluck-clucked her concern.

I stared at her in shock. I'd unknowingly changed her thoughts, her ideas, her very emotions. I didn't know how exactly, but I knew with absolute certainty that I'd somehow connected with a normal mind and made that person think what I needed her to think.

But all I did physically as she examined me with concern was to grab one corner of a sheet and help make the bed. She grabbed the other corner and we made up that bed while I tried to come to grips with what had just happened, but I shook so hard I could hardly work.

Halfway through, Riley entered. His eyebrows rose as he stared from Nurse Fiona to me as she smiled kindly and told him how helpful I was even though I no longer officially worked at the clinic and was somewhat tired.

His eyebrows rose even more as she shooed me away from the bed because 'my boyfriend' was here to collect me and we deserved an evening together instead of working in a busy clinic. She smiled beneficently as we left.

"What just happened?" Riley asked after dragging me from the room as fast as possible.

"I don't know, exactly." We almost ran to my apartment where I tried to explain. "What I was needing her to think became her thoughts."

"It's part of the mind reading thing?"

I shook my head. "No, what happened in that room was different. It's never happened before." To anyone in the entire community of mind readers back on Earth as far as I knew.

He chewed his lower lip thoughtfully. "But it started with you reading her mind." I'd told him what Nurse Fiona had tried to do and he'd listened without interrupting. "But the mind reading thing changed into something else when it became a life-or-death situation. Is that what you're saying?"

"I guess so." I shivered.

He stared at me intensely. "Anna, I always knew you were special. Now I know just how special. And I believe you have a very extraordinary gift."

"I read minds. That's all and it's not extraordinary in my community."

"You did more than just read a mind today. You changed Nurse Fiona's thoughts. I suspect that makes you special even among your own people."

I shivered. "I don't want to be special. I'm already different from everyone else on Nova One. I don't want that difference to be exaggerated."

"Too late. It already is." He reached for me, and I curled into his warmth and wished I could stay there forever.

CHAPTER 8

JAKE AND MOIRA CONNECT – FINALLY

They always returned to their makers on a preset schedule that had been programmed into them when they were created. They downloaded their information and then went back into space to learn more that they would also bring back to their makers.

Sometimes only one of them returned at a time. Other times, several returned simultaneously.

One time three of them returned to their home planet simultaneously only to discover that it was no longer there. It had been destroyed. It was gone.

———————•●•———————

Traveler thought wearing a leash was a privilege. Moira and I got in the habit of taking him for walks. We became a fixture in the town square where we usually shared a meal of fish and chips, though he seemed to get mostly fish and we got mostly chips.

After our meal, we liked to stroll behind the

greenhouses because we enjoyed the peace and solitude. We were usually the only sentient beings in that very large, quiet, well-planned green space crowded with the stubby trees Nova One seemed to specialize in both in and near the greenhouses. It was a jungle without the heat and humidity.

None of which mattered to us. We simply liked the ambience. The greenness of the place. The stillness. The light filtering through all those leaves. The silence.

Until one day it wasn't silent. "Hi."

I looked up. Then I looked at Moira because the 'hi' was mostly directed at her. I merely happened to be in the area.

"Hi." Why'd her voice squeak just because she was looking at the Security guard who'd let Traveler aboard Nova One? Jake. His name was Jake. I quickly read Moira's mind, something I seldom did because I respected her privacy. But the guard had been interested in her and, by her reaction then, she was just as interested in him. So I listened.

She was remembering the fear when she first saw the guard – Jake -- holding her kitten, knowing he had the power of life or death over her tiny friend. That fear returned. She wished she could hide Traveler but she couldn't. It was too late, he was hopping around at the end of his leash.

Jake joined us on the path and matched our steps, strolling in an unconcerned way beside us but a bit closer to Moira than me and behind Traveler who was straining at his leash. It was as if the Security guard didn't notice how his sudden appearance had turned our peaceful evening into one of confused feelings.

"Why are you here?" Moira gulped. "Have you

changed your mind about Traveler?"

He shook his head. "I noticed the three of you and thought I'd join you for a walk."

Traveler, hearing us, came back and climbed Jake's leg. Moira reluctantly surrendered the leash when it became too tight to keep hold of and he took it and Traveler rode his shoulder and purred happily. "I told you before I'd not turn him in. He's a nice kitten."

"You could have changed your mind." Moira still didn't totally trust Jake. After all, he was Security and that made him the enemy according to her way of thinking.

He snorted. "Not likely." He gave Moira a look that said she should know better than to think the worst of him and on his shoulder Traveler echoed that look. His big eyes said he trusted Jake completely and Moira should too.

She hunched her shoulders. She wanted to trust Jake. But her kitten was important. "Sorry." She looked down and scuffed the ground.

"Don't be sorry. It's a natural enough assumption." Jake stared into the greenery. "It happens all the time. I'm Security and people seem to recognize that about me even when I'm out of uniform."

I gave a hiccup of laughter as the last vestiges of Moira's fear dissipated and was replaced by interest in Jake as a man that was equal to his interest in her. I dropped back to give them privacy but they didn't notice. They were too interested in each other to know I was around.

I looked Jake over and decided that of course people recognized a Security guard. The upright posture. The short haircut. The general air of confidence and the way military types see everything in one quick glance. "Imagine that," I murmured to myself when my hiccups subsided enough that I could speak if anyone cared to listen – which they wouldn't -- but my insides were still giggling.

Jake harrumped and patted Traveler who decided he'd ridden Jake's shoulder long enough and jumped down to go exploring to the extent his leash would allow. Then he explored a bit further. Then he tugged hard at exactly the right angle. And slipped free. And looked back at us, his kitten face inscrutable. Then he disappeared in the thick green stuff.

The face of the supposedly cool and unflappable Security guy showed shock. "I let him loose." Then he shouted, "Follow him!" Before he finished yelling he was after the tiny kitten, plunging into that tangle of green. Moira and I followed and we three humans soon found ourselves in foliage so thick I was unable to see. I could hear them but the greenery distorted sound and I couldn't place either kitten or humans.

Surely a starship jungle wasn't large enough for a kitten to get lost in. Except it was. Until I heard a frightened meow. It came from overhead so I looked up and there was Traveler, near the top limb of one of those stubby trees. A short tree as trees on Earth were measured, but high enough that I couldn't reach him and the branch he was on swayed dangerously.

Neither could Jake reach him after he and Moira both crashed through the undergrowth to reach us. He tried but every time he almost reached Traveler, the small kitten backed away until he was close to the tallest branch and it swayed under his slight weight. Jake frowned. "I'm too large, too heavy. It'll break if I try to climb it."

"I'm smaller." I said, "I'll go."

"I'll give you a boost."

But even though I'm light enough that the branches held my weight, every time I reached for Traveler, the little kitten backed further away until he was on the highest branch. It swayed dangerously and that frightened him. He meowed loudly.

Jake stared at the feline. "Moira, he's your kitten. He'll come to you." Before she could answer I slid down and Jake grabbed Moira around the legs and lifted her towards the tree. In some corner of my mind I realized that Jake was one strong dude if the easy way he lifted her was any indication of what the rest of him was like. And good-looking. And nice because he was into rescuing kittens. Moira was going to be one lucky woman when the two of them finally realized they were meant to be a couple instead of two people circling each other warily while Nova One sped through space.

Jake was right. Traveler came to Moira almost immediately, purring and skipping onto her shoulder and tucking his head into her neck as if nothing out of the ordinary had happened. As if the whole thing had been an accident. As if he'd not intentionally slipped free of his leash.

I tried to read his little cat mind but failed because I'd not had much experience in reading animals' minds but I was pretty sure that if I could read his thoughts, he'd be laughing out loud.

"Huh!" Jake said, staring hard at Traveler when we were all finally back to normal, having brushed foliage off each other and made sure Traveler was secure in his harness, after which we found a table at a pizza place.

Jake glowered at Traveler, who meowed politely. "Do you suppose he was waiting for me? Did he know this was his chance to escape because he knew he could get away if I had the leash?"

Moira examined her kitten and tried to still her hormones while not knowing whether they were going haywire because of the rescue or the rescuer. The tiny kitten or the good-looking Security guy. Watching her, I considered the pizza on the table in front of me and wondered how fast I could eat a piece so I could say I'd had enough and had things to do so I could get out of there and let them have a little privacy.

I stuffed a piece of pepperoni pizza in my mouth as Moira said, "He does look a little too innocent for it to have been an accident."

"You should know," was all Jake said in a flat, droll voice, referring to Moira's life as a rebel.

I left as soon as I finished that slice of pizza, reading their minds as I walked away. Moira tried to eat without taking her eyes off her kitten and pretending not to stare at Jake who she wanted to devour with her eyes.

Then Jake said, "What say we bring the rest of the pizza to your place and finish it there? So we can enjoy it instead of watching a kitten sized escape artist to make sure he stays put?"

They brought the pizza and a couple root beers to Moira's apartment. I'd already reached my own place and was glad I'd sprayed the mind-block everywhere so I wouldn't hear what was going on. Because I was pretty sure it had little to do with cats and a lot to do with Moira and Jake. At least, I hoped they were finally getting around to realizing they cared for one another, no matter that Traveler was a kitten worth talking about.

To make a long story short, they got married eventually and I was Maid of Honor. Their new apartment, one for a married couple, was still on Deck Five so as to be close to our work and turned out to be close enough that Moira and I still got together often. Riley hinted that maybe we should be next but when we actually talked it over we decided we weren't ready yet. I wasn't ready. The time wasn't ripe. The mind-reading thing still loomed too huge.

Eventually Riley and Jake became friends. Moira, to no one's surprise, decided on Security as her career path and she and Jake eventually became a team. Moira, the rebel became one of the people she'd avoided most of her life.

They were curious why I left health care. It seemed the logical thing for me to continue since Riley was a doctor. But they never asked and we never told them the real reason because doing so would involve telling them that I could read minds and I wasn't ready for anyone beyond Riley to know that about me.

I didn't have to read their minds to know what they thought of me being part of the First Contact team because their expressions said it for them. I was possibly a bit unhinged. But they never said anything out loud or asked why I'd chosen such an unusual career path.

Shortly after their wedding, Nova One entered hyperspace. The quantum entangled communication system didn't work as efficiently as before hyperspace, not for most of us, anyway. The shielded communication room near the Bridge and the one on the Bridge itself worked fine but were off limits to most colonists. So my chats with my family stopped. I missed them but often thought of them on Earth as I flew at break-neck speed through the space between the stars.

And so our lives settled into a routine and time passed uneventfully. We became complacent and life remained comfortable as Nova one reached and then passed the half-way point to our destination planet, accelerating steadily as we streaked silently through space.

Until all hell broke loose.

CHAPTER 9

METEOR STRIKE

Three of them returned at the same time but instead of their home world all they found was a ring of debris circling their star. Here and there in that debris they found pieces and remnants of what had once been a thriving civilization. But their planet itself was no more. Their home planet was now a dusty circle around a star among the billions of stars in the universe. It was gone and without their makers they no longer had a purpose.

———— • ● • ————

Living on Nova One was like living on Earth because the builders had deliberately created an Earth-like habitat so we'd be comfortable for the years we'd spend in the space between the stars. But we occasionally wondered about the planet we were headed for that astronomers said should support life because they were sure it was truly Earth's twin. Whenever we talked about that distant planet, we always wondered in an uncurious manner when we'd finally arrive.

It never occurred to us that we should have wondered *if* instead of *when*.

The day we learned about the '*if*' started like any other. It was Disembarkation Day in remembrance of the day we left Earth because we were starting a new civilization and wanted our own celebrations, and someone decided the day we left Earth should become a holiday.

People were everywhere. None of us had to work so the four of us decided to go shopping and check out the pods along the perimeter of the square. They were survival pods in case of a disaster. They were equipped with food, water, oxygen and sleeping gear to keep us alive and in reasonable comfort until we could be rescued.

Except nothing bad ever happened and everyone came to think nothing ever would. At about the half-way point of our trip between the stars, some business types had convinced Bridge to let them use the safety pods as pop-up shops to sell stuff because they were large enough and all the emergency stuff was stored in cabinets along the walls. Useable space, they said, so why not use it?

They pointed out that if there was ever an emergency the pods could still serve their function. People would just have to shove merchandise aside while waiting for rescue. Not that there'd ever be an emergency. What were the odds? Practically zero. In the meantime, entrepreneurs could conduct a little business and practice for when we made planet-fall and became real colonists with a need for real businesses.

So the captain made it happen.

As we four strolled along the pod-businesses we passed one filled with floaty looking tops in all the colors of a rainbow that looked like they'd fit both Moira and me. We weren't the same size – she's taller than me and I'm skinny as well as short – but the floaty tops looked like they were the one-size-fits-all kind.

The pod was empty. The owner must be on an errand, but the pod was open so the owner must not care if people went in to check out the merchandise. So we looked at each other, shrugged, and meandered into the shop where Moira and I immediately began checking out the floaty rainbow-colored tops. They really were quite nice and we discussed which we'd ask about when the owner returned.

Then it happened.

A loud bang came with no warning and was immediately followed by an explosion so hard the deck beneath our feet moved and bucked. Then everything went silent. It was a deadly, stunning silence. Then we heard the worst sounds of all. The ominous whisper of air escaping followed by the klaxon scream of the emergency siren.

There wasn't a drill scheduled. It was real. I tried to see what was happening when I realized the others were staring out the door. I turned to see where they were looking. And gasped.

What had been a peaceful scene moments earlier was now something out of a horror movie. Confusion. Destruction. Smoke. Broken furniture and walls and greenhouses. I looked past all that to where there should have been fake blue skies and saw only blackness. The blackness of space.

There was nothing between that blackness and us. No fake sky, no pretend clouds and most important, not the hull of our starship. Nothing but a gaping hole where that hull should have been.

Slowly, then faster and faster, things rose into the air and began floating. I stared, unable to look away as debris was sucked towards that black void. Towards space. And the klaxon siren kept screaming.

Then something else happened. The door to the pod slammed shut.

"Breach!" Jake yelled. "Meteor! There's a hole in Nova One ."

Moira went into Security mode. Just like that. One second she was trying on a green and orange top and the next she was at the door, pounding on it, trying to open it. "Those people need help!" Objects in the park rose faster as they floated towards the gaping hole in Nova One's side. "We've got to do something." But the door didn't budge. It was built for exactly such situations. It would keep us safe even against our will.

Jake and Moira failed to open the door as the first of the people in the park were pulled towards that black void. I heard their screams. Not physically because the door was too thick for sound to penetrate. But I heard their thoughts. Their cries for help. Their wish to live. Then I heard silence as they died. I didn't know which was worse, their cries or that awful silence.

I couldn't handle it. I ran to the door and tried to open it. Like Moira and Jake, I failed. I tried to get my fingers into the crack between the door and wall but there wasn't enough space for my fingernails. But I tried anyway, scrabbling at the line separating the door from the wall.

Riley knew I could hear those screams. He pulled me away from the door and hid my head in his shoulder, whispering words I couldn't hear because all I could hear was the screams of those poor people followed by that terrible silence.

Moira and Jake gave up and for a moment we just stood there knowing there was nothing we could do. No one we could save. It was only by a freak coincidence that we'd been in the pod when the meteor hit. A thing of floaty tops.

And still people died. We watched them grab furniture to keep from from being sucked into space but as the air pressure dropped, they lost consciousness, their grips failed, and one by one they disappeared into the black void beyond Nova One's hull.

Then, in what was probably mere moments and seemed like hours, as the pressure outside and inside the starship equalized, everything stopped moving. Furniture, people, plants and pieces of glass. Everything. The few remaining lights winked out as power died and Deck Five became a black, empty cavern. Silence reigned.

"There's no air out there."

"We'd die if we could open the door."

"We're stuck until rescue teams get here."

Riley loosened his grip on me. He'd been holding me so hard that my skin was white and I didn't know if he was trying to help me or himself deal with what had just happened. "I'll call so they'll know where we are." He spoke into his comm implant but stopped almost immediately as his face drained. "The coms are dead."

"It doesn't matter. They'll come looking. By now they know what happened."

"Unless they think everyone died." No one spoke. We stared at one another and beyond the pod to the death and destruction mere feet beyond the sturdy door that had saved our lives. I didn't need to read minds to know what everyone was thinking.

We were alive. But how long before we were rescued? How much canned air did our pod contain? Would it be enough? Would we still be alive when they arrived? I stared through the door that had slammed shut and saved our lives. "How long, do you think?" No one answered.

Rations were in the walls of the pod along with water and a rudimentary bathroom. We opened the cabinets and checked the survival supplies. "Mattresses and sleeping bags so there must be enough oxygen for an indefinite stay." I read the list of supplies and instructions on the inside of the door. "All the necessities of life for up to ten people and there are only four of us so no problem. We just wait."

So we waited. We waited minutes, figuring rescue squads would respond ASAP. No one came. Then we waited more and still no one showed up. That time multiplied and we told each other that rescue squads had to check the apartments first because if there were any survivors there they wouldn't last as long as people in emergency pods. We were safe. Those other people might not be. So there was a reason for the delay but our turn would come.

"Maybe there aren't any rescue squads. Maybe everyone is dead. Maybe we're the only ones left alive."

I set my mind to range as far as possible to listen for thoughts and heard the cacophony of yells and instructions that accompanies every disaster though I heard nothing specific to our situation. "I'm sure Deck Five was the only deck affected." Because I couldn't tell Moira and Jake how I knew there were still people on Nova One.

Riley knew I'd heard people. "I think Anna's right. The meteor only hit in one place and Nova One was designed for such situations. Even if there was more than one meteor, the entire ship won't be damaged. We'll be rescued. We just have to wait."

So we waited still more. I rolled out sleeping bags and we all slept fitfully until we gave up pretending and unfolded a table and chairs and sat around and drank coffee and stared at one another. We tried to talk but eventually even gave that up because there was nothing to say. Nothing good, anyway.

There were sounds. We jumped every time we heard a creak or snap. Nova One was wounded and she groaned and snapped as she hurtled through space with a gaping wound in her side. The indestructible Nova One was hurting badly.

We took turns standing by the door to watch for rescue parties but could see little because everything beyond was the black of space and starlight wasn't bright enough to make out any details. We had light in the pod because it was self-sufficient. And we saw no lights carried by rescue parties.

When we couldn't stand looking at each other any longer, we found separate corners to sit in as we waited some more until much, much later I heard voices. Not out loud, I heard them in my mind but they were close. I sat up straight and gave a gasp. "A rescue party. They are looking for survivors."

Moira asked, "How do you know? I can't see anything."

"I hear them." I pretended to be surprised. "Don't you?" Then I pretended some more. "My hearing is better than most." I closed my eyes and concentrated, raising my head and not breathing in the pretend effort to hear better. "They are on Deck Five. I'm sure of it."

"We have to get their attention." Light from the pod could be blocked by the debris that was everywhere "They can't see us."

We were energized. We crowded around the door. Someone grabbed a flashlight and pointed it in every direction possible. Flashed it on and off. We screamed and pounded on the walls even though we knew it was useless. We prayed. We did everything we could think of to get their attention.

I listened to their thoughts. The rescue team headed straight towards the apartments. They passed us without noticing us. They stayed at the apartments a while and then left. They never checked the pods. "They probably think the pods are destroyed. We were close to where the meteor hit."

"They are leaving." I wanted to scream. Hit something. Do anything to make those people know we were alive.

"How do you know?"

"I can't hear them anymore." I could but their thoughts receded as they made their way back to the upper decks with the few survivors from the apartments. "They think we are dead. They won't come back."

There was silence for a long time. Then Riley said simply, "Then we'll save ourselves."

"How?"
No one answered.

CHAPTER 10

WE FACE REALITY

Their home world was gone. Destroyed completely. The fact was incomprehensible and when the truth of what had happened sank in, they didn't know what to do. Their original programming had not prepared them for this possibility. The three that had returned at the same time got together to consider their future now that their makers were gone. They considered the vast universe and their place in it. They spent much time thinking.

———— • ● • ————

After a while, Jake spoke. "There might be a way." He explained further. "The front door shut when the pressure dropped. But the whole idea of the safety pods is that there's a back door leading directly to the center core and that core was built to withstand just about anything, including stray rocks from space." He continued. "We were given a tour before colonists were allowed on board."

Riley said, "A rescue party reached the apartments. The only way that party could have gotten here was through the core."

I went to the back of the pod where the outlines of a second door were visible if you looked closely enough. "So all we have to do is open this door and walk to another deck?"

Jake nodded and the others joined me. "It's not supposed to open from inside – a safety thing – but it might be possible."

Except when we tried the door it didn't open. We tried again. Still no luck. I looked at Jake. "Is there a trick to opening it?"

"There's an electronic lock and a panel that controls it." He opened a panel next to the door and swore. "The panel is dark and that means the controls won't work." He slammed the panel shut. "We're trapped."

After a moment of dead silence during which we contemplated what little future we seemed to have ahead of us, Riley gave me a look that said he wanted to talk privately. I blinked back that we should say we were tired and head for a corner and a sleeping bag and mattress. We did so and, when we were curled up together he whispered, "You can open the door."

"Me? No I can't. I can read minds, I can't open doors."

"It's electronic. That's a kind of communication and communication is your specialty. If there's even a flicker of power left then those lines of communication may still be viable and I know you can read them and unlock the door."

"Impossible!" No one had ever done such a thing. I couldn't read a mindless machine.

But as I rolled away from Riley and curled into a ball, I couldn't forget his words. What if he was right? What if electronic communication was similar to the way a human mind works? What if there was enough resemblance to thought that I could actually do what he suggested? Read the combination of the lock?

"Remember Nurse Fiona?" Riley's voice was soft so the others wouldn't hear. "Remember how you made her think what you needed her to think? Maybe you can do that with the lock on the door. Make it open itself." Then, after a moment, "If it doesn't work we won't be in any worse situation than we are now. But if it does work – if you can unlock the door – then we'll save ourselves."

I turned to him. "What about Moira and Jake? They'll think I'm insane."

"So what if they do?" He touched my hand. Just touched it but that was enough. "Maybe this is the time to tell them about you. What you can do."

"No!" So loud Moira and Jake looked our way. I scrunched deeper into the sleeping bag. "I don't want anyone else to know."

"If we don't get out of here it won't matter whether they know or not. If we do get out, I doubt they'll go shouting about your mind-reading ability to everyone they meet. They'll be so glad to be alive they'll keep any secret you wish."

I said nothing for a long time, during which I looked around the emergency pod. The walls that were so thick no one would hear us. The doors that wouldn't open. And I took a deep breath and said, "Okay."

Riley rolled to his feet in one fluid motion and pulled me up beside him. Then he turned to Moira and Jake and said, "We have something to tell you guys."

Moira's eyes went wide. "You're pregnant?"

The thought was so unexpected that I laughed as I shook my head. I actually laughed. "No. This is different. Very different."

"Then what's your big secret?"

I gulped. "Riley thinks I can unlock the door. I don't think I can, but he's talked me into trying."

"You're a locksmith?"

"No." I took a deep breath and said it for the second time since boarding Nova One. "I'm a mind reader and maybe I can read the lock's mind and convince it to open itself."

In the following moments it was clear that they did indeed think I was insane and they only came around when they checked out Riley's face and saw that he was deadly serious. Then they didn't know what to say so they said nothing. Just stood there slack-jawed and stared at me.

Riley took my hand and led me to the panel. He opened it and stepped back. "Do your thing, Anna. I know you can do it. You can get us out of here."

I tried though I didn't know how to communicate with a piece of metal. There'd been no classes on locks when I was a kid. But I sent out mental feelers and did my best.

I actually got something. Feelings. Sensations. "There's air on the other side. Pressure. Safety. If I can open it, we can walk out of here."

"It's five inches thick."

"You can do it, Anna." Riley moved close, unsure

whether he'd be more help by being close to me or by leaving me alone. I didn't know either but some instinct told me to reach out to him. To use him though I didn't know how I'd do such a thing or whether my instinct was true or simply a wish to hide behind him.

For whatever reason, I touched him. Felt his warmth. Then felt that warmth trickle from his body into mine and I instinctively knew how to use that warmth. I closed my eyes and sent my mind out of my body with more force, thinking how we'd die if I failed.

I felt something. I didn't know what I was sensing but there were wires and patterns and pathways in my mind that made no sense but I followed those paths hopefully because I knew that if I followed them far enough and made the right turns and twists that I'd somehow end up where I wanted to be.

But where was that? What was my destination? I didn't know and was about to back out and open my eyes and say the whole thing was a mistake when suddenly I saw a mental picture of a bright light shining through an open door. And there was an audible click. And the lock moved and the door swung open.

"You did it!" Riley's voice said he'd hoped for a miracle but hadn't truly expected one. But a miracle had just happened in that pod and when I opened my eyes, I found myself staring at a slack-jawed Moira and Jake and a door that had opened about a foot, enough that air rushed into the pod from the central corridor of Nova One.

"We can get out," was all Moira said, awe plain in her voice

Except we couldn't.

Riley shoved the door and tried to open our

pathway to freedom. Nothing happened. He frowned. Tried again. Still nothing. "Something's blocking it."

We all helped the next time as Moira muttered that we'd sort out the mind-reading thing later when we were safe. That time it moved a fraction of an inch. "Must be something big."

"So we shove harder."

We tried. Nothing worked. The door opened a few more inches and then stopped. "Let's get a little rest and then try again."

We sat around and opened the stores of supplies and gulped water while we stared at the recalcitrant door. Then we tried again.

It moved another inch or so. We cheered. But when we pushed again, nothing happened. Riley reached around the door to feel what was pressing against it from the other side. His face went gray. "I don't know what it is but it's huge and heavy. A part of a wall or a large machine."

"The door is as open as it's going to get."

"We can't get through."

My next words came out unbidden. "I can."

I felt their eyes on me. "You are the smallest one here," Moira said finally. "You can fit through the door and go for help."

Jake handed me his flashlight. "You'll need this."

Riley said simply, "Stay safe and come back to me." I thought about the questions about me that he'd spend the next few hours answering as I approached the door, took a deep breath, and examined the darkness beyond.

CHAPTER 11

THROUGH THE CORE OF NOVA ONE

They would have mourned their lost makers if they'd been created with emotions, but there'd been no need for emotions when they were made. But they did have intellect which was similar enough and enabled them to know what had been lost. They eyed the debris spread across their star system and knew they were all that was left of a great civilization.

———•●•———

I was never brave. I didn't want to come on this journey in the first place and now I was about to take another, equally dangerous trip through the damaged core of Nova One. But with my head held high I considered the slender opening in the door, trying to look as if I knew what I was doing and was happy to be doing it.

I squared my shoulders, stood as tall as possible, and squeezed through. I almost didn't make it. I twisted and turned and tried to turn into Jell-O and somehow, miraculously, I made it through.

Once on the other side, I turned to see what was blocking the door. As I examined it, I realized that in no way would we have been able to open it further. An entire wall had collapsed against it, canted just enough to allow us to open the door slightly. An inch less and I'd not have been able to get through.

Then I looked in both directions, seeing nothing but darkness and wondering what I'd encounter on my journey. If I'd reach safety. If I'd find help. If I could navigate the total devastation that was now Deck Five.

I started walking, shining the flashlight and picking my way through the debris that was everywhere. The light from the escape pod that shone through the partially open door gave me additional courage until a huge bookcase rose before me. When I went around it, it's bulk blocked the light and left me in complete darkness except for the narrow beam of the flashlight.

I was alone. Truly alone and afraid. I went around something even larger than the segment of wall that had fallen against the door and wished someone else had been able to squeeze through the door. Anyone.

Keep moving, I told myself. Keep going. Peoples' lives depended on me. Me, the coward who wanted to stay on Earth. But as I slowly made my way through the core, I realized that if I hadn't come, I'd not have met Riley. Not have learned I could do more than I'd thought, perhaps more than anyone back in my community of mind-readers could do. Who knew, I thought as I circumnavigated a distorted security check point, I might end up a different Anna than the one who boarded Nova One all that time ago. Maybe.

I picked my way carefully, going around things I couldn't begin to recognize, hoping I was still going in the right direction, glad of the raised numbers that told me where I was. Those numbers comforted me.

The elevators didn't work but there were stairs that wrapped around them and led from deck to deck. There was also a ladder that could be climbed if both elevator and stairs were destroyed. I hoped the stairs would still be functional because the distance between one deck and the next was huge and the fall if I missed a step would be very bad. Probably fatal. Which thought made me realize that if I was indeed a different person now that new me wasn't much braver than the old me.

The stairs were blocked. Of course they were. I inspected the ladder and took that first step, thinking of the tree Traveler had climbed. I told myself it was the same thing only with rungs. Then I took another step. And another.

I stumbled and almost fell but I caught myself and hung on and told myself everything would be okay and, miracle of miracles, it was. Then I climbed another step and stopped long enough to pray that I'd make it safely. Then I was on the next level where I lay on the deck and flashed the light around.

Deck Six was much like Deck Five. Lots of destruction but, as I examined it in detail I realized the damage was less. Encouraged, I checked the stairs, hoping I'd not need to use another ladder to reach the next deck.

Then I stopped as something hit my mental senses and hit so hard I almost doubled over because I sensed – something. Not a person. Not a lock or any other object I recognized. But—something.

I went totally quiet. I stopped moving. I stopped breathing.

I strained to hear anything but there were no sounds in that inky blackness beyond the sounds of a wounded starship. No sense of another person. But there was – something.

I couldn't wrap my mind around it. It was unfamiliar but it was very real. I felt it. Somehow.

Then I heard a whisper except it wasn't exactly a whisper and I couldn't figure out whether what I heard was an actual sound or a mental one. Because what I heard weren't quite sounds and the voices weren't quite voices and the thoughts weren't quite thoughts. But they were -- something.

Then whatever I sensed was gone. I searched mentally for someone – anyone – that might have whispered in the dark but I sensed no one any more. Heard no one. Felt no presence after all even though moments before I'd been sure someone was there. Some *thing*.

I started shaking. Wrapped my arms around my middle but it didn't help. Looked for a place to sit until the shaking stopped. The stairs to the next level seemed intact so I dropped to a step and sat until I was able to control my body. I can't remember if I cried. I probably did because I wasn't brave and didn't care if I cried because no one was there to see.

Or was someone? Was whomever had whispered watching my tears fall? Without a mental or real picture to tell me what those entities looked like, I simply thought of them as 'whisperers.'

The flashlight made going possible so when I was able, I rose and continued on, only now I went faster because I was running from something unknown and possibly dangerous. I took the stairs to the next level at a run, where I ducked beneath a chain across the stairway that looked like it was there to prevent people from going down to the damaged levels.

Then I heard voices. Real voices, not whispers. I heard actual people talking and I ran towards the sound. A middle-aged man with thinning hair and a hint of a pot belly saw me. He examined me, top to bottom and back again, and frowned because it was easy to see I wasn't at my best. Scuffed clothes, tangled hair, who knew what else. He asked, "What happened?"

"I'm from Deck Five." His eyebrows went up. "There are people who need help."

"You can't be from Deck Five. We got the survivors a while back." His face closed. "There weren't many, but we found a few in the apartments."

"We were in a pod."

"The pods were destroyed."

"Ours wasn't. Only we couldn't get out." I explained and he drew in his breath and called for help. In what seemed like moments a fully equipped rescue team was asking questions. What pod were we in? What number? Where was it? What blocked the exit? Was anyone hurt?

I answered as best I could. Even before I finished people disappeared down those same stairs I'd come up armed with flashlights and ropes and everything needed to rescue my friends. I watched them go numbly. Someone shoved a chair towards me and I sat down. Hard. The man who'd first talked with me stayed nearby, keeping an eye on me.

I was safe and so would the others be. I should

have rejoiced. Instead, all I could think of was the whispers I'd heard while in the core. I turned to the man beside me. "Who was down there a little while ago and what were they doing?"

He pointed to the chain blocking the stairs. As if I hadn't seen it. "No one. That's why I'm here, to make sure no one goes past that chain."

"Someone was there."

"You saw someone?" I explained that I couldn't see anyone or make out their words but I knew they were there because I'd heard something. He shook his head. "There was no one. You probably heard Nova One creaking. Probably will last until repairs are made."

"Okay." I clearly didn't believe him and his expression said I'd be checked for emotional trauma as well as physical injuries. I didn't want to argue so I just sat there and thought about how, somewhere in the dark recesses of Nova One when there wasn't anyone around, I'd heard something. I'd heard whispers or something like whispers.

It took time to move an entire wall away from a door, which was what had to be done for the others to be freed. Equipment was brought down the partially missing stairwell and then it had to be positioned. Shielding had to be passed through the narrow opening in the door to protect those inside from the explosion that would free them. So it was a long wait to see Riley, Moira and Jake and the longer I waited, the more I thought about whispers.

My self-appointed caretaker distracted me from what he thought must be simple trauma by asking generic questions and pretty soon I was the center of a small knot of people clamoring to hear my tale including a reporter for Nova One's usually boring news program. She was so excited to actually have news to report that she hopped from one foot to the other until settling down to await the coming of the rest of the group so she could see what they had to add to the story.

Then they were there. Riley and my eyes connected but the crowded conditions prevented a reunion because everyone, it seemed, wanted to hear what had happened. They talked over one another and jostled for position and generally were loud and pushy and interested and wonderful because they were real, live people like me who lived and worked on Nova One. Most of all, though, they talked. They didn't whisper.

Moira and Riley and Jake answered questions but I was the one who'd gone through the dark corridors so I was the one that reporter wanted to talk to. Not saying anything would make me stand out so I had to say something but before I could open my mouth someone placed a gray and white cat in Moira's lap. She screamed in joy to know Traveler had survived in the apartments and had been found along with the few survivors there. His meows had been heard.

But even as Moira cuddled Traveler and the reporter snapped picture after picture of her and Traveler because pets make wonderful pictures and eventually, when a medical type took us away from the crowd to be checked out medically, followed by a debriefing by people in uniforms, the whispers in the dark were in the back of my mind.

Of course I didn't mention them to those medical types or the Security types who asked a million questions after the medical types cleared us to be questioned. Not a single word.

CHAPTER 12

WHISPERS

Should they deactivate themselves? They debated that course of action and decided there was no reason to do so. Their home planet had been destroyed but they still existed. Surely that meant something. The thing was, they told each other, they'd been created for a purpose and just because their makers no longer existed didn't mean their purpose was no longer valid. So they contemplated possible futures and eventually decided to continue doing what they'd been created to do.

———————— • ● • ————————

Riley and I lagged behind on our way back to our apartments. Farther and farther back until we could talk without Jake and Moira hearing. I turned to him. "There were voices. I heard voices."

"I knew something was going on. You were too quiet and you looked odd and we didn't think it was the walk that caused it. The others knew something was wrong but none of us said anything." Then he asked, "What did you hear?"

"I don't know."

We'd been given new apartments on Deck Six until Deck Five could be repaired. Someone must have thought Riley and I were married because we were given the same apartment. Riley's eyebrows went up when we realized we'd be co-habiting. I said nothing but somewhere in my gut I thought this was the way things should be.

We got together with Moira and Jake after settling in. Moira dropped to our couch and said, "So, Anna, about this thing Riley said you can do." Her voice was skeptical. "I know you unlocked the door but I still can't believe it's for real."

"It's true."

Next came the same question Riley had asked when I'd told him I could read minds. "What am I thinking?"

This time my answer came promptly and easily because my emotional attachment to Moira was that of a friend. "That you don't believe I can read minds but there's no other explanation."

"Yep. But that's what anyone would think when someone says something so – unusual." She tipped her head towards Jake. "What's he thinking?"

I giggled. I actually giggled. "Same thing with the caveat that he hopes I haven't been eves-dropping on you two in private." I looked straight at Jake. "I haven't. That would be rude." Jake turned red and slid further down into the couch cushions. "And don't worry about it. I never do that."

I read Jake's next thought. "And, yes, I can turn it off if it's important to do so." Not completely true but no reason to trot out the lessons I'd learned as a kid on how to ignore thoughts you don't want to hear. It's not perfect but it works well enough unless there are so many thoughts crowding in on you that it's like a flood and you're drowning, which often happened on Nova One. Too many normal people who didn't block their thoughts. But that wasn't the case with just two friends who deserved a little privacy.

Riley explained about the whisperers and that it was now urgent that they know what can happen when people read minds, even beyond unlocking a door. "Anna doesn't know if she heard actual sounds or heard them in her mind." Moira and Jake sat up and took notice. They were Security and this was their area of expertise.

"I still don't know what it was. Whispers is the closest I can get to describing it."

"Wind maybe?" Moira considered possibilities. "The sound of space? We've never heard it before because there's never been a breach before."

"Not space. Not wind. Real voices with real thoughts only I couldn't tell what they were thinking." I gave them a moment to absorb what I'd said before continuing. "I just know they were thinking about something. Discussing it."

I thought back to that moment in the core when I'd heard the whispers. What it had been like. The utter foreignness of it. "Their thoughts were strange. Different" I shook my head. "I don't know how to explain it any more than that."

"How different?" I gave Moira and Jake credit.

They'd got past the mind reading thing with lightning speed when confronted with something greater. Potentially more sinister.

"I don't know." I took a deep breath. "But I have a thought strange as it may sound." Another breath so I could say it. Could get the words out. "I'm not sure they are human."

"Aliens? You think aliens entered Nova One through the breach?"

"It's the only thing that makes sense."

"Are they dangerous?"

"I don't know."

"Have you heard them since then?"

"No. They are silent." I tried to hide my frustration. "But not gone. They are still there, I sense them but all I get are scraps. Seconds or less." The silence was deafening. "The thing is, I think they do more than whisper. I suspect they also talk because I think some of what I heard wasn't just thoughts. It was words said out loud but softly because they didn't want to be heard."

They looked at each other. "So we should listen too? Is that what you're saying? You want us to help you?"

I nodded. They said they would but their thoughts said they doubted they'd hear anything. Mostly they thought that if something was happening on Nova One I was the only person who could figure it out because I could read minds.

Finally, after a long, long, pause, Jake said, "God help us if they are aliens and are unfriendly."

CHAPTER 13

WE REACH OUR DESTINATION

They would continue exploring the universe but they'd do it together for their own edification instead of to add to the knowledge of a civilization that no longer existed. Most of all, though, even though they'd not found intelligent life and didn't expect to find it anywhere, ever, they'd keep looking because the Universe was large and the possibilities were endless and finding intelligent life in the universe was one of the reasons they'd been created.

———————•●•———————

The breach was repaired. Thousands of robots worked nonstop until it was as if the breach had never happened. Deck Five once again became a place of life and living and greenhouses and apartments filled with people. We moved back to apartments that were replicas of the ones that had existed before a meteor destroyed the originals. Riley and I returned to two apartments instead of the one we'd shared on Deck Six because someone had thought we were married but people on Deck Five knew we weren't.

I visited Riley that first evening of our return. I knocked. He answered. "You don't have to knock. You know that."

"I know." I stepped in and closed the door behind me. I looked at Riley and he looked at me. Waiting. Wondering what I wanted. Why I was there. I cleared my throat. "I was thinking about us."

His eyebrows rose. "Us? As in us being two people in a relationship?" He gestured towards the couch and we sat without touching. "What, exactly, were you thinking about us?" His face was conflicted. "Good or bad?"

"Good." I reconsidered. "Maybe good. Depends."

The eyebrows went higher if such was possible but he gave no other indication of emotion. "Depends on what, exactly?"

"You." I cleared my throat again. Why was I having a problem speaking? Okay, I'm not the best speaker ever to exist but I could usually manage okay. But not then. "Me. Us."

He considered me gravely. "Depends on you. Me. Us." His eyes narrowed. "Interesting subject." He said nothing beyond those words. Instead he waited. Just waited.

"I think it's time."

He blinked. "Okay. Good to know." He paused for a long time. "Time for what, exactly?" A smile ghosted across his face. "I can't read minds, you know. You have to tell me. With words." Then because he's Riley, he added, "When you're ready," because he always said that, ever since that first conversation with my father. Now he leaned back and folded his arms and waited some more. One of Riley's best qualities is his patience. He's got tons of it.

I blurted it out. "Time for us to get married. If you're ready. If you still want to."

He was still so long I wished I'd stayed silent because it appeared he'd changed his mind. I was mortified. Then he said, "I've been ready since I first offered to father your children." He paused and added, "But you weren't ready then and I accepted that."

"I'm ready now."

He cocked his head and examined me closely. "Why?" Because he knows me, Riley does, and he knew this came from somewhere.

"It was the trip through the core." I wanted him to know. Needed him to know. "Things happened that I hadn't expected and I was afraid I might die without knowing what it was like to be married to you and I don't want to take any chance on that happening in the future, not ever, especially not with whisperers wandering about Nova One so I want us to get married as soon as possible." I took a deep breath after that long run-on statement. Then I finished with, "If you still feel the same way. If you want to marry me. If you want to do it soon."

"You have to ask? Really? You don't know?" He started to laugh. Soon tears were running down his face and he bent over and laughed some more and pretty soon I was laughing too because I'd been so dramatic and almost incoherent that it was hilarious. "Let me give you a hint."

He reached for me and I didn't leave that night or any other until we were married with Jake and Moira in attendance, saying it was about time and they'd almost given up on us ever being smart enough to do what they'd done long ago. Then we got a larger apartment and settled into our lives on Nova One and I learned what it was like being married to Riley. It was great.

I concentrated hard on being married. Riley diplomatically asked about those children I should be having but I said I wasn't ready yet. One thing at a time, I explained. I wanted to learn how to live in the normal world and that was hard, not to mention there were unknown things wandering Nova One and whispering. Those whispers could be dangerous.

His eyes dimmed a bit but he said nothing, simply nodded that the whisperers were enough to deal with now and I was glad again for him because he didn't push even a tiny bit.

I hoped marriage and getting to know Riley all over again would make me forget the whisperers. It didn't but nothing untoward happened. No aliens appeared. No contact was made. I almost wished I'd never mentioned them. But they were there, I knew they were, I could sense them, and even being married to Riley couldn't push them out of my consciousness.

Every so often I sensed their presence strongly enough to know they were communicating with each other about something important though I could never interpret their thoughts. Then one day Moira and I were strolling through the greenhouses with Traveler who loved them and was allowed in them after that one incident only wearing a harness he couldn't get out of. We found a bench and sat and watched Moira's cat wander as far as his leash would allow.

Suddenly Moira went still and put a hand on my arm to indicate I should remain quiet. She cocked her head the way people do when they are listening to something hard to hear. Since she was obviously listening, I did too. And heard the whisperers. I didn't sense them. I actually heard them.

She turned to me, her eyes wide as saucers. "I hear them, I really do. I hear your whisperers." She went silent again for a long time as we both listened to whispers in no language we recognized. "You were right all along. But I have no idea what they are saying."

That was the beginning. Eventually all four of us could hear them once we all knew what to listen for. The whispers were quiet enough to not have been noticed if not for my hearing them that first time. But still nothing untoward happened so we never told anyone else about them.

Time passed. And still more time. The whispering didn't increase. Neither did it stop or lessen. Now and then, though, it changed. Occasionally we could make out words. Not sentences, not ideas. Just words. "Perhaps the whisperers aren't aliens after all."

We decided they must be people who spoke a really odd language and that was reassuring. Nova One hadn't been invaded during the hull breach. The whisperers were human beings though no amount of research could identify their language.

More time passed. The whispers became a part of our daily life but we somehow managed to push them to the backs of our minds because we were too busy living our lives to concern ourselves with something we couldn't see and could barely hear and definitely couldn't understand beyond a word now and then. Especially since they weren't aliens after all.

Nova One sliced through space as she'd been created to do. Like everyone else, we traced our path through space on displays created to follow our trip but life on the starship had become so normal that it didn't seem to matter where we were headed or that eventually we'd reach a place that was just a dot on the star charts. Arrival was too far in the future to be real.

Bridge sent probes to that future planet but we ignored the findings because they didn't have anything to do with us. We were informed the planet was livable but we just shrugged at the news. The gravity would be a bit heavier than on Earth, we were told, so Nova One gradually increased its gravity to match and our air soon had a bit more oxygen because that, too, was adjusted for our future reality. But it was all done so slowly that we didn't notice or pay attention. Why would we?

And then it happened and we weren't ready. Nova One reached her destination. We arrived and that changed everything.

We began orbiting our future home. The viewing rooms filled to overflowing with people wanting a glimpse of the new planet though no one could actually go planet-side until the captain gave the order and he seemed in no hurry.

Then one day I got a call along with the rest of the First Contact team. I curled against Riley that night and was surprised that I was only doing so because I wanted to feel him next to me instead of because I needed reassurance.

I was surprised that I wasn't afraid. Had I grown in bravery? Had the trip through the core changed me more than I knew? I spent the night feeling his stalwart presence beside me while wishing I could read his sleeping mind and wondering if I was merely drawing strength from him and would feel fear when that presence was no longer close.

The next morning we First Contact people assembled on the Bridge and formed ranks and received instructions. "You head for the planet's surface in two Away teams." No name yet for our new home so it was just 'the planet.' "Second team goes only after the first returns." So if something happened to one team, there'd be a backup. That wasn't said in so many words but we knew it had been planned that way.

"Don't worry, everyone will get a turn taking a good look-see at our new home and you'll all have plenty of time to explore." The speaker, a stocky Security type was all confidence and positivity. "No civilians until we're sure it's safe. Then the scientists go down and do their thing. Colonists will be the last to set foot on our new home."

CHAPTER 14

A NEW HOME

After plotting their future, the three of them set out on a journey with no schedule and no baggage because they'd been created to maintain, repair, upgrade, and redesign themselves as needed. Stars, planets, asteroids and the dust of space contained everything they needed to keep

themselves going forever. As they headed away from what had once been their home, they expected there would be no end to their journey, merely a continuing accumulation of knowledge.

———— • ● • ————

We spent the rest of that day peering down at the planet. On the Bridge we could see easily. It had a viewport that wrapped around the entire operations center. The rest of the Nova One viewing rooms, those for colonists, were so crowded there was little chance of seeing anything except someone's back. Actually arriving at our destination had caught everyone's attention. Big time.

Our new home didn't look impressive. Small continents of green with snowy white mountains that were hardly larger than the islands that dotted the oceans. We saw no birds flying through the air and no animals moving on the ground, not even when the view finder panned in as close as possible. Like ten feet above the ground. The blue oceans were a better place to look for native life, the biologists said, because life begins in the sea and maybe just hadn't yet made it to land beyond the extensive and lush looking green landscape. But when the view finder was panned in to inches from the water, we still saw nothing. No fauna at all.

The consensus was that there might be no native life forms beyond plants so there was little concern about potentially intelligent natives. After all, they said, plants aren't sentient, therefore, they aren't dangerous.

I was in the first Away team. So were Moira and Jake. Riley would have liked to go but doctors weren't a priority. If something jumped out at us we'd either survive or die but if the worst happened medical science was unlikely to help in an alien environment.

We went through clouds and someone said that was good because if we crashed the debris would be hidden from Nova One. "They don't want our deaths to be broadcast live and in full color."

Someone else added, "Because we're expendable. Our remains will be swept under the table but the second expedition will be given a ticker tape parade."

Our new home grew larger as we got closer. The green stuff that resembled grass or weeds was everywhere but it was hard to tell what those green things were until the shuttle shot over a mountain – or a really high hill, it was impossible to tell the difference from the shuttle – and there we saw still more, very tall green things. Not trees, but close enough.

We disembarked and stepped onto a new, virgin planet, Security in their silver and black planet suits and the rest of us in blaze yellow. Not that we needed colors to identify us. Every Security type carried weapons that were cocked and ready. No one else did.

There was no fanfare, no speeches, just a group of people there to do what we were trained for with Security fanning out in every direction, on alert with weapons we could only hope would be adequate if unfriendly local life forms appeared and we First Contact people failed to make peace with the natives.

It turned out that those awesome weapons weren't needed. There was no sign of life beyond the green stuff that was everywhere. There was an incredible variety of shades of green and different sized green, growing things but everything we saw was green. Just green. Every single living thing. Everywhere we looked we saw plants and nothing else.

"It's creepy."

"This place hasn't yet evolved animal life."

We shivered uneasily and told ourselves we'd get used to the overabundance of green foliage. Then we gathered green things in the bags we'd brought for that purpose though we'd expected some of them to carry insects, birds, and other forms of life. And we determinedly didn't mention again how creepy it was.

Except it was also beautiful. As we walked among the greenness and brushed our hands over the tips of green, growing things we decided we could get used to it. We hoped it wasn't poisonous. Besides, we told one another, we had animals on Nova One that would love the endless pasture and we'd plant some colorful flowers to make it more home-like.

After a while, Security said the planet seemed safe, even going to such lengths as to sling their weapons over their shoulders instead of carrying them at the ready and then they spread out to investigate further. I decided to take a look-see a bit further away and wandered over a hill where I saw – of course -- still more green things spreading out in all directions.

I remembered my childhood. I'd loved living in the country and this was similar. More importantly, it was a planet instead of a starship. When I was hidden from view behind that hill so no one could see me make a fool of myself, I raised my arms to feel the wind that was fundamentally different from the mechanical airflow on Nova One.

Then I turned my face to the sun and said a short prayer because we'd reached the place we'd been heading towards for so many years that we'd forgotten we had an actual destination. All that time we'd been heading for this particular, specific planet. Not the next planet or the one after that. This planet and no other.

We would stay here, I thought, as I turned completely around to take in the view. We would colonize it no matter what. Danger and death be damned. Not that there any danger from a grassland that stretched as far as I could see.

For a long time we all meandered about aimlessly. One very thin First Contact team member who was examining the green stuff we were walking on had an Irish lilt that all those years on Nova One hadn't managed to change. He turned completely around several times, looked at the green stuff under his feet and took in the horizon in every direction. "It's the Emerald Isle all over again."

He pointed to the ground and then to the trees or what looked enough like trees to pass for them if you didn't look too closely. "It's all green. It's Ireland on steroids. Every frickin' thing on this planet is green."

Someone examined a small, green growing thing carefully and then pointed to the sky. "Even the clouds are green."

"Those aren't clouds. That's pollen. Guess pollen is the same everywhere, even on stray planets light years from home."

A man whose wife was a biologist kicked the green stuff and watched bits of it fly in every direction before falling gently to the ground as the green cloud reached our small group and enveloped us, blotting out the sun. "This planet reached the stage of photosynthesis and stalled."

A short, plump man wasn't daunted in the least by green anything. "All we have to do is provide a little direction and guidance and turn this planet into humanity's second home. We'll have those animals and birds here in no time along with whatever else we choose."

The only thing we didn't take samples of were the thorny bushes that seemed to be everywhere. We were too conscious of the orders not to let our planet suits be compromised to take a chance with the thorns. But a bit of everything else ended up in the sample bags.

We returned to Nova One with those specimens and the news that the planet held no intelligent beings and seemed safe enough to allow larger groups to investigate our new home. For short visits, of course, wearing planet suits and in pairs for safety's sake.

The entire starship erupted into cheers and all the shuttles were put into service as soon as possible and the main body of colonists – anyone who was interested and that was everyone on Nova One – went down in groups and got a look-see at our new home. Our totally, completely, entirely green world.

CHAPTER 15

DEADLY GREEN

They continued on through the Universe, learning, growing, experiencing everything possible. Until one day they noticed something unusual. Something different. Something made by intelligence as they'd been programmed to recognize it.

———— • ● • ————

Our new world was all plants. No animals to attack us in the middle of the night. It was safe.

Except, as we soon learned, it wasn't safe at all.

Moira, being Security, had accompanied a group to the planet's surface. Trips were popular even though they were closely monitored and there were all kinds of restrictions in place to make sure nothing untoward happened.

According to Moira, one woman kept saying she wasn't afraid of this new place. She kind of swaggered and said she wasn't afraid of anything. Mostly, though, she told everyone who'd listen that she was a chef who created great dishes like some people created great pictures. She was that good, she said. The thing was, people who'd eaten at her restaurant agreed. Her food was amazing.

She was going to the planet's surface to expand her menu with local items, and she made no secret of the fact that she desperately wanted some of that green stuff visitors kept bringing back in those little, transparent bags that they gave to the scientists. Nothing had been poisonous, she said, not a single thing and everything looked absolutely delicious.

She'd not have chopped them up and put them beneath a microscope. She'd have put them in a salad instead of sending them to the laboratories. So she could hardly wait to get her hands on large bunches of salad makings once she reached the planet's surface.

Because Security was still cautious, no one was allowed out of sight alone, especially people who wanted to gather forbidden samples. Every civilian was paired with someone, and Moira ended up being paired with the talkative gourmet cook. For safety's sake, Moira told her. So they suited up, stepped out of the shuttle, and wandered behind a hill.

Moira soon learned they were behind that hill so no one could see the cook take off her helmet in order to more carefully examine the greens she wanted. Moira wasn't fast enough to stop her as she hung her helmet on one arm, put her hands on her hips, looked around, and said, "I can feed the entire starship for a year with what's in this immediate area."

"Put that helmet back on."

"Not a chance. There's nothing dangerous here.

Just a beautiful salad waiting to be made."

The adventurous chef sniffed, cautiously at first, and then with a smile that grew and grew and grew. She increased the amount of air she took with each breath as Moira tried to get her to replace her helmet. No such luck. The chef just shook her hair with one hand until it blew in what was by then a slight wind while she cut greens with the other that she stuffed carefully into what was a rather large bag. "It smells wonderful here. And warm. And everything we've been dreaming about. And look at all this delicious green stuff."

The wind picked up still more as Moira considered body-slamming the chef to get her to comply with regulations, but the chef evaded Moira's clutch and shook her head even harder as her hair flew every which way in real air instead of the manufactured kind on the starship. Moira told me she envied the look of sheer enjoyment on the woman's face but didn't dare admit how she felt because orders were orders and helmets were required.

The wind blew harder, and the chef's hair blew across her face and she laughed in sheer delight. But the wind also sent clouds of the green pollen flying from the nearby things that might have been trees.

The chef was busy gathering greens as she and Moira watched one such cloud approach. The green cloud was concerning. Moira frowned. Not likely to be dangerous but you never knew about such things.

As the green cloud reached them, Moira decided enough was enough and grabbed the recalcitrant chef's helmet and plopped it on her head. But before she could fasten it down, it was torn from her grip as the chef grabbed it and threw it as far as possible across a field.

Moira swore. "You have to wear a helmet."

The chef stuck her tongue out and laughed and picked more greens. Then she sucked in an especially deep breath as the green cloud reached them, taking in as much as possible and closing her eyes in ecstasy. The pollen was perfumed, she said, and she loved it.

Then she coughed. Shook her head, blinked pollen from her eyes. And coughed again. Tried to wave the pollen away from her head and failed. And coughed again.

That time she coughed up blood. Not much and she looked in surprise at the blood on her hand until, realizing what caused it, started looking for her helmet. By then Moira had retrieved it and jammed it on her head and this time the cook didn't argue because she was suddenly afraid.

But it wouldn't fasten right because it was cracked from being thrown and by then the wind was blowing so hard that some of the green pollen crept through the cracked neckline. She couldn't avoid breathing it. She coughed again. That time there was more blood.

Moira screamed into her helmet comm. "Medical emergency!"

Medics were there as fast as they could run in the awkward planet suits, but it was too late. They tried everything they could think of. Nothing worked. All they could do – all Moira could do – was watch the chef die a horrible death, choking on her own blood, the little air she managed to gulp being full of the very thing that was killing her. Beautiful, aromatic, green pollen.

Her body was respectfully carried to the shuttle. Moira picked up the mesh bag of greens, wishing it didn't exist, knowing she'd throw it away as soon as possible, wanting to throw it as far away as she could but this was a new planet and they'd been ordered to bring back everything they took with them. Every. Single. Thing. No polluting, they'd been told, no destroying a new and pristine planet.

On Nova One, there was a suitable service, attended by so many people that most had to stand outside the chapel. The body was composted as per protocol and a stumpy tree planted in her honor.

As Moira and I left the service, we overheard a group of scientists talking quietly among themselves. What had happened was a tragedy, they said, but informing. It had taught them some very essential things about this new planet. Sobering things. One thing especially.

As they talked, they wondered how long we'd have to wear planet suits in our new home. The green stuff was deadly, they said, judging by what had happened, and it covered the entire planet.

They guessed we'd have to wear them forever.

CHAPTER 16

I MEET THE WHISPERERS

They saw a projectile, long and sleek and metallic. Beneath the thick covering of regolith that protected the inner metallic core, they sensed life. Movement. Machinery. And thoughts. So they followed it, knowing they'd finally found the most important thing they'd been seeking all that time. Intelligent life. But the projectile was shielded by that regolith and the thick layer of metal. There was no way they could penetrate it without destroying it in the process and they'd never do that. Until one day, a meteor struck the projectile and put a hole in one side. Then they could enter. So they did.

* ● *

The horrible death of the colonist who removed her helmet had everyone on edge, me included. But not enough to remain on Nova One. I was a mind-reader, after all, and wanted to hear what colonists were thinking about their new home. Where better to find out than on the planet's surface?

The main problem was that everyone who wanted

to visit the planet could now do so and that was everyone, which was a big deal because there were only so many shuttles and thousands of colonists who wanted to make the trip. But eventually the day came that Riley and I could ride a shuttle to the planet as tourists instead of me going for work.

Riley hadn't been planet-side yet and was eager to see our new home. Besides, he still had that male ego that made him think he had to protect me, and I was going so he figured he'd best go too. Really? I was the First Contact person, he was just a doctor. I should be protecting him and I let him know it. He laughed.

We boarded the shuttle. I was so eager I couldn't sit still as we penetrated the clouds and headed towards a prearranged landing spot. We exited the shuttle and stood about, looking and feeling foolish. What to do now? Where to go? I hadn't been a tourist before and didn't know how to act.

Riley gazed around. "Looks like an interesting planet."

"It's pretty much the same everywhere."

"This is my first time so I do want to take in the sights and I'm sure it's not all the same."

I sighed. "Okay. Where should we go first?"

"There are ponds all over this area according to the maps I checked before boarding the shuttle. Let's see what they are like." He did know a lot about the planet. Probably more than me because he'd actually gone to the trouble of learning a bunch of things. I figured it was the scientist in him. I go more for the intuitive approach.

He pointed. "According to the maps I read, there's a pond over that hill. What say we find out what it's like."

We climbed a short but very steep hill. I'd not done any climbing on my first trip. I soon learned that it took skill to navigate this landscape without slipping on the thick carpet of green vegetation. We slid down the other side of the hill and found ourselves beside a small, crystal-clear pond.

I dropped to the ground and examined the water as the ever-present pollen floated through the air. I wished I could swish my hand through it, but the planet suits didn't allow for such familiarity with the landscape. So I sighed and stood up once more and looked around. And then it happened.

I heard something. A faint, barely discernable whisper. I listened harder, checking Riley to see if he, too, heard it but he was busy checking out the green fields that stretched beyond the pond. I closed my eyes and concentrated on the faint sounds. The whisperers. There were three of them. They were hiding from us, but they were nearby, I could sense their nearness.

The hair on the back of my neck stood up. I nearly puked in my excitement. I was about to see the whisperers at last. To discover who they were. To confront them. Riley noticed my excitement. His eyes narrowed and I mouthed that the whisperers were nearby. He remained calm, the scientist to the end. He led me to a boulder where we sat and considered the situation.

I took a deep breath and thought how to tell him what I wanted to do without alerting the whisperers to the fact that I knew they were near. "I want to look for something interesting."

He nodded that he knew what I really meant.

"Let's go."

We silently made our way between two low hills. We could see well even though pollen gave the entire area a greenish hue. I grabbed Riley's arm when I heard more whispers to get his attention. The thoughts were louder, which meant they were closer. Riley stopped as I reached out mentally with all of my ability, with everything I'd been born with and everything I'd been taught until, so suddenly that it came as a physical shock, I connected with them mentally. Actually connected.

That had never happened before. I'd always just listened. Now whatever my mind had touched backed away instantly in a kind of shock that mirrored my own, blocking further contact. "I connected with them. They know I can read minds."

Riley went very still. "Your call, Anna. Is it safe or not? Do we stay or go?"

"Stay." I listened and got more slivers of thought. "They are curious. I don't think they are dangerous."

"Curious about what?"

"I don't know."

"Then we just keep moving and finally find out who they are."

As if on cue, there was a movement behind the nearest hill. There was no animal life on the planet so the movement had to be the whisperers. But we were careful. We moved slowly towards the hill.

What happened next, happened quickly. There was another movement. Running. Three figures running so fast that we saw them only briefly before they disappeared. Three people. So they were human as we'd figured. Except –

"They didn't wear planet suits." I stared at Riley.

"Shorts and tee shirts." Neither of us could comprehend what we'd seen.

"The pollen should have killed them. But it didn't."

"Why not?"

The voices in my head went silent. Whoever they were they were gone. So we returned to Nova One knowing the whisperers were real, they were human, and they could survive where no one else could.

I returned to the surface again as soon as possible. I wasn't sure what I expected to find but I'd seen the whisperers once and perhaps I could repeat that sighting. I would go alone because I was the only person who could communicate with them. I didn't even want Riley along. If I connected with them – and that was a huge 'if' – I didn't know what I'd do but wanted to be able to act quickly without having to explain what I was doing to someone who couldn't read minds.

I got a seat on a shuttle the next day because by then most colonists had been there at least once and the pressure for seat space was low. I sat in comfort during the trip through the ever-present clouds and was glad the insistence on staying with a partner was no longer adhered to so I could look for the whisperers alone. Yes, I decided, I'd come a long way from that insecure girl who hadn't wanted to leave Earth. In my eagerness to meet the whisperers in person and alone I hadn't even had time to be afraid.

I found the path Riley and I had taken before, the one with a pond surrounded by hills. I told myself that just because I'd seen the whisperers there before didn't mean they'd be there that day. But with no better idea, that was where I went. And I sat down on the same boulder Riley and I had sat on and listened and watched and thought how foolish I'd feel at the end of the day when nothing happened. And sure enough, I heard nothing.

Until I did.

I heard whispers.

I snapped to attention and heard pieces and parts of words spoken low by people who knew they'd been heard before and were trying not to be heard now. I closed my eyes to concentrate more fully. I let my mind roam. I stretched myself to the limit searching for faces to match the voices.

Did I actually have those enhanced powers Riley thought I did? Could I locate someone with the power of my mind? I decided to try. I sent my mind high above the hills and over the pond and then I mentally flew higher and higher still until I was flying between the tree-like things and the clouds. I was doing something I'd never done before. But was it working?

It was. I located them. I saw the whisperers. Not physically but I sensed where they were. Which hill they were behind. Three of them in a circle, discussing something. Pointing now and then towards me as I sat on a boulder with my eyes closed. They knew I was here. Did they also know that I'd located them and was reading their thoughts?

I'd have to run to get to them before they could disappear as they'd done the day before. So I stood up and ran. Around the closest hill and along the river that wound through the area until I reached the next hill and started around it because that's where they were. I sensed it. I knew it was the right place. Not far. All I had to do was run faster and I'd find them before they could disappear.

Except it didn't happen that way. I tripped. I should have seen the shale, should have known it was loose rock because it was the only part of the landscape that wasn't green. It was gray and on this planet where things grew everywhere possible, a lack of green meant loose rocks.

But I was so intent on finding the whisperers that I didn't pay attention to my surroundings and as I dashed across those loose rocks they went out from under me and I crashed to the ground. I hit hard. I felt rocks scrape along my body.

I picked myself up more frustrated than in pain because I feared that the time spent falling and getting back up would be enough for the whisperers to get away. I was afraid that even if they hadn't already sensed my presence – which they probably had -- the sound of rocks sliding and my body hitting the ground had made enough noise that now they definitely knew I was coming.

At least I hadn't broken any bones. I could still run. But as I reached the end of the loose shale and ran flat out I felt a difference. Something was wrong. I looked down at my planet suit and realized things were bad. Very bad.

My suit was ripped wide open. A tear began at the top of one boot and went all along the planet suit to my neck. It was a huge tear that left a large part of my body open to the air. But that wasn't the worst. Like the helmet of that first woman to die on the planet, the locking mechanism for my helmet had broken in the fall.

The wind of this new planet now blew freely into my helmet as it had done with hers. The perfumed air was wonderful and if I breathed it in, I'd die and if I held my breath I'd die anyway.

This new, green, beautiful planet would be the last thing I'd ever see. Soon – in mere moments -- I'd be writhing in agony and coughing blood until there wasn't enough left in me to keep me alive. Then I'd die. It had happened to that first woman whose helmet had malfunctioned. It would happen to me.

I'd been a coward most of my life but as that wind swirled around me I decided that at least the end of my life would be faced bravely. I drew in a deep breath, determined to get it over with as quickly as possible. As I took a second breath, I felt a constriction in my lungs and knew it was starting.

I kept my eyes open -- I'd look this planet in the face as it killed me -- so I saw them when they came. The whisperers. Three people running flat out around the hill and straight towards me, eyes wide and legs pumping in their hurry to reach me before I died.

In some corner of my mind, I thought how this was the ultimate irony. To finally meet the whisperers and then to die.

CHAPTER 17

I AM CHANGED

They quickly deduced that the intelligent beings in the projectile did not know of their existence. Like their makers, the beings in the projectile thought they were the only intelligent beings anywhere. But their makers had thought ahead to such a possibility and decided that, in an abundance of caution, their creations should not reveal themselves until such time as was deemed practical. So when they entered the projectile they changed themselves to resemble the beings already there. In disguise they began moving among those beings to learn more about them and they communicated with each other mentally in order to not be found out and as they learned the language, they spoke it quietly so as not to be overheard. They whispered.

———————•●•———————

The whisperers were there to watch me die. Would

they take pleasure in the fact that they could live without suits and I couldn't? Would they enjoy my agony? Would they laugh?

No, they would not because I'd die bravely. They'd not get a chance to enjoy it. So I stared at them unblinking as they closed in on me. I prayed to be able to stay upright as long as possible. To meet their looks with my own.

Our eyes met. There was no expression in theirs. Neither joy nor sadness. Nothing. Well, I decided, I knew how to express myself. I managed to stand almost straight even though the agony was beginning and I stared at them with all the serenity I could muster.

The first to reach me grabbed my helmet. Yanked it off. Looked at the others and nodded as if something was as expected. And leaned in close to me and said, "We'll fix you."

Then she leaned still closer and gently but firmly placed a hand over my mouth and nose so I couldn't breathe.

Why smother me? Did they hope I'd suffer more that way? I tried to shake the hand away but couldn't. I coughed but the hand stayed firmly in place.

As the other two came close, peering at me through those expressionless eyes, I felt the lack of oxygen hit and struggled unsuccessfully for air as one of them came closer still and touched my shoulder. I felt a slight prick. Then everything went black.

When I came to, I expected to be in Heaven. That's where you go when you die, isn't it? But if this was Heaven it looked suspiciously like the same, green planet I'd been on. And the three figures peering at me with undisguised interest looked suspiciously like the three who'd come to watch me die.

So maybe I wasn't dead. But if not, why not? How could I be alive after breathing in the green haze? I drew in an experimental breath and discovered I could breathe. Furthermore, surprisingly enough, I breathed easily. The air was perfumed and a warm wind curled around my body. A green, hazy wind. The same wind that blew ceaselessly across the plains and hills of the new, unnamed planet and killed people. I was immersed in that haze except somehow it hadn't killed me.

I looked around for an explanation but all I saw were three people staring at me with what seemed like purely intellectual interest. Then I looked at them more closely and felt a belly laugh coming because they were triplets. Identical triplets. Medium brown hair, medium brown eyes, medium brown skin, medium height. Medium everything. And all the same from top to bottom.

"Why aren't I dead?" I sat up straight and gave them the toughest stare I could manage.

"We fixed you." They stared back with those expressionless eyes. "Like we told you."

I checked myself. No planet suit but I saw it a few feet away. I reached for it with a foot and dragged it close and my mouth dropped in shock. No rips. None at all. "What happened to my suit?"

"We fixed it." They looked at each other and then at me with still no expression. "It's good now."

I flexed my arms and stared at the three of them. Hard. "But I obviously don't need it. I'm not dying after all so why'd you fix it?" I asked again, "Why?"

"If you don't wear your suit people will ask questions."

"True," was the only comment I could manage considering that by then, not only was I alive, I was in shock.

We stared at one another, three identical expressionless women and me. Until I couldn't think of anything more to say except to ask the question I hadn't asked moments earlier. "How did you fix me and my planet suit? And how long did it take?"

They looked at one another and communicated without words. No one but a mind reader would know that they were communicating and it was hard for me to read thoughts that flew from one to another at dizzying speed. But they'd not blocked me, so I was able to pick up enough to get a general idea what they were talking about.

They were wondering how much to tell me. Could I handle the technical aspects of what they'd done? Should they dumb down their answers? Would I keep their secret? I listened and realized that it was essential to them that they remain hidden. Secret.

As they'd always been. All those times on Nova One. "Is that why you whisper? Because you're afraid of being overheard? Because you're hiding from something?" They turned back, mildly surprised that I'd read their minds. "I've heard your thoughts for a long time so don't lie to me."

"We don't lie," one of them said in that flat, expressionless voice. "Ever."

"Then will you explain what you did to me?"

As we continued the stare-down, they sent thoughts flying among themselves until they reached a consensus. They turned towards me and the first one said, "We changed you."

The second said, "We had to."

The third finished with, "It was the only way."

I examined as much of myself as I could see and didn't see anything different. One of them said, "We changed the part of you that was unable to breathe this planet's air."

"You *what*? How?" I still didn't see anything different.

"We changed your DNA."

I was speechless. I tried to wrap my mind around their explanation and failed. "How? And how'd you do it so fast?" I looked around us. "It's still today, isn't it? How long have I been asleep?"

"Minutes by your time measurements."

They'd changed my DNA in minutes with no laboratory or equipment. "Am I still me?"

"You are still you but you can now breathe the air on this planet."

"You changed my DNA? Just like that?" I failed to wrap my mind around what had happened as we stared some more, me with increasing bewilderment and the triplets with no expression at all. "How? Please tell me."

They consulted again. "We studied humans so we knew how to change your DNA."

"How'd you learn?" My husband was a doctor but neither Riley nor any other doctor on board could do it so easily and quickly with no side effects.

"When we were made we were given knowledge. We accumulated more over time and still more about you while on your starship. So we knew what to do."

I opened my mouth to say something but stopped as I realized what they'd said. The important part. So I shut my mouth again until I forced myself to ask a different question using carefully thought-out words. "You said 'made.'" I made my next question crystal clear. "You weren't born? You were made?"

They answered in unison with no expression at all. "Yes."

I thought a long time before asking my next question. "How, exactly, were you made?"

"The usual way."

I took a deep breath. "Okay, you were made the usual way. But forget that for a moment because it's going to take me some time to wrap my mind about that little detail and tell me, where exactly, were you made?"

"In the factory."

"You were made in a factory?" They nodded in unison. "What kind of factory, exactly?"

Again, they answered in unison. "The usual kind."

I didn't know what to say. I was flabbergasted. And at that exact moment, the klaxon sound calling us back to the shuttle blasted through the helmet speaker and all I could do was reach for my suit again and start to pull it on.

And that's when I noticed my skin.

I was green.

CHAPTER 18

I GET TO KNOW SOME ROBOTS

The intelligent beings in the projectile were like their makers in some ways and not like them in others so they agreed with their makers that caution was best, at least until they knew more about them. They hoped for a close encounter with them eventually but weren't sure if it would turn out well considering the beings seemed unaware other intelligent, sentient beings existed. They did not know how the beings would react to such unexpected news. So they kept apart from the beings while keeping alert for an encounter that would be a first for both them and the beings.

———————— • ● • ————————

I read their minds. It was easy now because they'd evidently decided not to block their thoughts. They were thinking that my new skin color would make me the center of unwanted attention when the shuttle reached Nova One and I removed my planet suit. It would be a problem.

They said, "We changed you. We are responsible for your new color."

I examined my green skin and wondered what the future would hold for a green person. Me. "It's best for me to hide but I can't do that in the shuttle bay when we take off our suits. It's crowded."

Their thoughts flew so fast I could hardly follow but then they spoke. "We have learned about hiding since boarding your starship. We know how to hide so we can help you hide and return safely."

"How?"

"We will bypass the shuttle entirely and bring you back to Nova One ourselves, thus eliminating the need to be seen by other humans during your journey or in the shuttle bay."

"Won't work. They won't lift off until everyone is accounted for, including me."

They consulted again. And again their thoughts flew so fast I couldn't keep up. Then they turned to me with another idea. "In that case we also will ride the shuttle. We will make planet suits and wear them and look like everyone else. We will stay close around you and hide you."

"That won't work either. Too many people instead of too few."

There were still no expressions but after more consultation they said, "Then we will return to your starship our usual way and be in the shuttle bay when you arrive. We'll be in planet suits so as to resemble everyone else and we'll take ours off along with everyone else but we'll be close enough to you that no one will see your skin color."

One of them sighed. "Humans are complicated." A sign of emotion. I'd wondered.

It worked exactly as they predicted. As soon as the shuttle docked and we headed for the suit lockers they appeared and crowded around me. When our suits were hung up we all walked lockstep to the door leading from the airlock and then onto the main part of Nova One.

We did get a few stares from people who wondered why we were all crowded so close together. But we didn't make eye contact with anyone so no one asked questions. "We'll change your DNA back to what is normal for you as soon as we reach a private place," they told me when we finally reached my apartment complex.

"No."

"No?" They seemed to think I didn't understand. "Green skin will attract attention. Normal human skin color won't." But I knew exactly what I was saying. I'd been thinking about nothing else since realizing I could breathe the planet's air.

"If green skin means I can be on the planet without a suit then I want to remain green." I looked from one of them to the others. "Do you know what that means? How monumental it is?"

More consultations. "We can see that the ability to breathe unencumbered is beneficial." A questioning look came on their faces. Another hint of emotion. "We can change all humans so they can also breathe the planet's air."

Would the colonists want that? If they wanted to colonize the planet we'd come so far to live on being able to breathe the air safely would go a long way towards realizing that goal.

"So you will tell other humans how to become green? Green skin isn't exactly usual. We suggest you think about it first."

Two people strolled past and the triplets as I'd come to think of them closed protectively around me. After they turned a corner, I said in a low voice, "I'll explain everything if you'll come with me. I want you to meet some people."

"The other listeners?"

"You knew we were listening?"

"Of course. And occasionally reading our thoughts as well as our speech."

All the time I'd been listening to them they'd been listening to me and, occasionally, Moira, Jake, and Riley. "I want the others to know about you. Who you are. *What* you are." I stroked my green cheek thoughtfully. "And to know that you can make it possible for them – and for everyone on Nova One – to breathe the air of this planet." I took a deep breath and said what I was thinking. "We'll see what they think and go from there."

They conferred. Discussed what was happening. And as they discussed I realized something. Knowledge was being given and received by all of us on an equal basis. No hiding. No whispering. But as we stood there, I realized something more. Something I thought must be odd for such capable, thinking machines. They were unsure of themselves. Why?

I backed off mentally as I'd learned to do in such situations, far enough to see it from a distance. And knew that there was more than just an exchange of information happening. There was feeling. Emotion.

As I realized that I also intuitively knew they'd never felt emotion before because I could sense their uneasiness at the strangeness of it. They'd not been created to be emotional. But somehow, they now were emotional beings or were becoming so. Again, why?

They'd copied our physical structure when they made themselves look like us and perhaps that somehow made them like us in other ways. Could that be it? I heard them wonder about this strange thing that was emotion in their fast-thought mode in that hallway as we appeared to be four normal human beings, one of whom was green.

Later Riley, Moira, and Jake were pretty much blown away by the whisperers who weren't whispering anymore because they had no reason to. Who they were. What they were, which we all decided after tossing ideas back and forth, was robots, though robots so far advanced from those we were familiar with that there was no true comparison.

We asked for their names so we'd know what to call them. They explained they didn't have names because names weren't needed and their makers' system to differentiate them from each other was so different from anything we were accustomed to that we wouldn't comprehend it any more than their makers would comprehend the human system of naming.

We explained that we needed some way to refer to them so, since they resembled each other identically, we eventually called them the Triplet robots and named them Robot One, Two, and Three. They were agreeable.

"Now we shall change the Anna's green skin back to what's normal for her," they said in unison and we knew we'd have to get used to them talking that way.

I shook my head. "I was thinking more along the lines of you changing all of us so we can breathe on the planet." After a pause I added, "Because it was wonderful. Freeing."

"Won't that cause consternation among other humans?" This time only one robot spoke. Robot One, I thought, though it was impossible to tell them apart.

The group was silent for a long time before responding with various thoughts. Jake finally said, "Maybe we should wait a bit before changing all of us. See how people react to a green Anna and then go from there."

Riley wasn't sure that was a good idea. "I worry about Anna if we do that. People can be nasty." But then Riley is always protective of me going back to when we first met and I actually needed protection. I didn't anymore but it was hard to convince him of that simple fact.

Moira, of course, was pure Moira. The rebel. No one ever had to protect her and if they tried she'd let them know their attention was unwanted, probably using words of four letters. "If anyone tries anything nasty, they won't succeed. There are four of us." She looked to the robots. "And maybe you three to back us up."

We were surprised by their answer. "We can protect you if doing so does not require that we harm another intelligent being of a similar technological level to that of our makers." They gave us time to think that over because human thought was slower than robot thought. Then they continued. "Our programming doesn't allow us to harm such beings. If we try, we'll be instantly disintegrated. It's in our hard wiring and cannot be changed."

"Can you protect someone if you don't harm the aggressor?"

"Perhaps, but we choose not to try so as not to disintegrate."

I rose. "Then it's time for us to tell Nova One what you are and that you can make it possible to live on this planet without planet suits and that means we must see the captain."

Our group of four humans and three robots headed for the Bridge, hoping we'd be granted time with the Captain and knowing we might not be. But it was time to let him know about the intruders that had been on Nova One and learning about humans ever since the meteor breached the hull.

CHAPTER 19

ROBOTS ARE INNATELY PACIFISTS

The captain listened to our story, examined my green self, admitted the value of being able to breathe the nearby planet's atmosphere, and agreed that three advanced beings with enhanced knowledge and experience would be valuable assets in settling our new planet.

I wasn't sure how much of our story he actually believed but his job required snap decisions in unique circumstances and his next words proved he was good at his job. "It'll take some fast talk to convince a few thousand people to become green." He raised his eyebrows and almost smiled, which said that in addition to being good at his job he enjoyed it. "It won't be easy but if you're up to it, you have my blessing."

He didn't leave us entirely to our own resources. Without another word he turned to the ship-wide speaker system no one could avoid hearing even if they wanted to. He spoke of green skin and explained that it would enable everyone to breathe without planet suits. He suggested colonizing was potentially impossible without being able to breathe the air.

Then he explained about the robots that were an integral part of becoming green. He called them the

Triplets and praised their abilities and emphasized that they were incapable of harming intelligent, technological beings like us.

Shortly after he spoke, our small group left the Bridge. The captain went with us. "To see how people reacted to my little speech," he said as he led the way to an elevator that would take us back to our original deck. "I have no idea how they took it but whatever happens will be interesting and I want to see how it goes down." As he told the elevator where to go, he added, "I want to know how they react because, knowing human nature as I do, I want to be prepared."

Nothing much happened beyond a lot of gawking and stares. I felt like a specimen under a microscope. But no one confronted me directly in either a positive or negative manner and eventually the captain decided he'd seen enough. "Nothing happening today. We'll see about tomorrow." He left and we continued our stroll through Nova One.

"The captain's gone so people don't have to be polite. Now we'll find out what people really think," Riley muttered. But the reactions of the colonists remained the same, which was no reaction at all. No one came up to us, no one spoke to us, no one made either a positive or a negative gesture. They merely stared.

The next day we went for a second stroll, per the captain's suggestion, to see what would happen after the colonists had a day to digest the idea of becoming green. We quickly learned.

There were a few guys in a tight knot not far from our apartments. They weren't smiling. When they saw us they went silent and the largest, an overweight man with muscles that matched his size, stepped forward and blocked our path. He spread his legs and folded his arms. Then he spoke. "We don't like the color green."

He poked a finger towards me and spoke loudly. "If you want to be a freak, that's your right. But if any robot so much as touches me or mine, I'll take it apart piece by piece and turn it into an eggbeater."

The robots thought the concept of a humans destroying them was humorous, humor evidently being an emotion they were in the process of acquiring as were all emotions. They found the urge to laugh interesting and decided laughter was a positive emotion. Then they decided the difference between positive and negative emotions was also interesting as they noticed that the man making the statement didn't see any humor in the situation. So they politely didn't laugh though they wanted to.

They tried to be polite since manners were something else they were learning. "Since you do not wish to be touched we shall not touch you," the robot closest to the man said and they thought that would be the end of the exchange. As they saw it, he'd made a comment followed by a response on their part. Their experience with human interaction said that was appropriate. Instead, the large man spit on the closest Triplet.

The small amount of human spittle was insignificant and the robots ignored it but we humans gasped and as we did the robots read our minds and knew they'd been insulted, which was another human emotion they figured they'd have to eventually incorporate into their new lexicon of emotions.

I mentally informed them that things were not

going well. My words led to another emotion new to them. Uncertainty. They decided that the emotion of uncertainty was unsettling and interesting at the same time. Then another man spit on the second robot.

Then a third spit on the third robot. The robots were unsure of the proper protocol in such a situation so they turned to me for guidance. Their expressions said they'd respond as I wanted them to as their mental communication said they thought emotions were a useful shortcut to communication but it could result in mixed messaging so they wanted me to instruct them. I mentally said that it was best to proceed with care when emotions were involved. With which our small group retreated to an area behind the greenhouses.

"It's looking bad."

"They are bullies. Not typical colonists."

"We'll find out soon enough if we keep walking."

If there were rational humans on Nova One, we didn't meet them that day but we did get spit on several more times and had tomatoes thrown at us. Especially at me. I was called names I'd never heard before and probably didn't want to know the meaning of. Afterwards we discussed what had happened.

"Convincing Nova One will be a slow process."

"If by 'slow' you mean 'never' I agree."

As we talked, the robots communicated mentally with each other and with me. I wasn't sure if they thought of me as their equal at mind-reading or whether they were merely being polite. I struggled to keep up though I did get the gist of their discussion and the ultimate decision that resulted.

I almost cried.

I said, "Don't go. Please don't leave." Everyone

went quiet. "We need you guys. Without you we may never be able to live on this planet." I explained to the others. "The robots have decided to leave because they believe they aren't wanted, and their programming won't allow them to stay in such a situation. They will deactivate."

Robot Two spoke. "Yes, that is true."

Robot Three said, "It's for the best."

One finished with, "Our presence is sewing discord which is a negative emotion, which is not desirable."

With which they rose. "Our makers took into account that this might happen if we ever found intelligent beings and revealed our presence. They created us with a protocol in our circuits to automatically activate should it be necessary." They headed for the door. "The protocol has been activated by our recent trip through the starship. Now we must leave."

With which they opened the door and left. I followed them to the airlock, trying without success to convince them to stay. Since they didn't need space suits or oxygen, they simply pressed the button to close the door to the ship and open the one to space. Then they walked off the platform, dove into space, and left.

CHAPTER 20

THE ROBOTS MAKE A CHOICE

I thought that was the end of our human-robot relationship but, as I later learned, instead of heading to outer space and continuing their journey, they fell to the nearby planet, found a green hill overlooking a stream and sat there because it was pleasant and as good a place as any to discuss their next move. Because even machines require plans.

For a long time they simply sat on that green hill beside that lovely stream. And sat some more. And experienced the emotions that were new to them that they'd discovered they liked, both because emotion itself was new and interesting but also because they liked the feel of it. And they finally admitted what they were thinking. "We do not wish to leave this place and the humans."

"But we cannot stay. The humans have rejected us so our programming will not allow us to stay. We should do what we were created to do. Explore the universe and acquire knowledge." But their makers no longer existed. So was their reason for existing no longer valid?

They thought further. Deeper. Wider. Mostly though, they thought differently, using their new emotions to process things in a new way and they decided emotion had made them aware that there should be more to existence than merely accumulating knowledge. They decided actual knowledge had little reason for existing unless it was put to good use.

This was a new concept for them and one that took some time to internalize because they were using emotion to process their thoughts. One of them finally said, "We struggle to deal with emotions. We do not know how to insert emotion into our equations and without doing so correctly our conclusions may be incorrect."

Silence grew as they considered that fact until one of them said, "There is a way." The speaker continued, "We can help humans with their problems because we have much knowledge and much experience with the universe. They in turn can help us with emotions because they have much knowledge and experience with emotions. It can be a fair exchange."

"But we can no longer be with humans because our programming won't let us stay where we aren't wanted and we can't go against that programming."

After another long pause, the third one said, "That is not entirely true." After a moment to give the others time to think, that one continued. "We are able to interact with the humans that accepted us."

The second one followed that line of reasoning. "It's true that our interactions with those humans did not cause us to self-destruct."

The third one concluded, "So we can interact with some humans without self-destructing. Just not with all of them."

They spent much time thinking about that while

watching the light of the planet dim as its sun disappeared behind the horizon and the living green carpet that covered every possible piece of ground curled into itself for the night. Even the wind stilled.

They let the emotion of the moment waft through them as they took in this new experience and wondered how they'd never before realized the intense beauty of the universe. "We shall communicate with those humans who accept us and ask if they wish us to stay."

"But they are surrounded by the humans who rejected us. How can we contact them without interacting with the ones that dislike us?"

One of them had an idea. "The humans come to the planet often. Eventually one of those we know will surely come. We can contact that human away from the others."

It was a workable solution except for one thing. "We are recognizable to all humans now, including the ones that rejected us. If they see us – and eventually that will happen – they will know that we are still here and will reject us again and we will be forced to leave."

"Unless we change our appearance so they will not recognize us."

It was a good idea. They discussed the details. "We must not look alike this time. Similarity attracts attention."

"What sex should we be?"

"Female again because human females are perceived as less threatening than males."

So before full dark arrived they resembled three middle-aged human females with different hair colors, different skin colors and different body types. Then they settled down to wait for one of the humans who'd accepted their presence to visit the planet. It was a long time as humans reckoned time before they recognized not one but two of the humans that had accepted them among those exiting the shuttle, but it did happen.

Riley and I were those humans. As we wandered about our new home I heard the thoughts of the robots. After I told Riley what was happening and got over my shock that they were still around, I mentally told them to meet us at the place where I had ruined my planet suit and they had repaired it and saved my life.

We were careful not to hurry as doing so would be noticed so it was a while before we all met. I wore no helmet. As soon as the robots appeared and we got over the shock of their changed appearance, Riley said, "Change me. Now. I want to take off my helmet."

"You will become green."

"I don't care. I want to breathe fresh air and enjoy our new planet."

So they changed him. One of them touched the back of his neck and put him to sleep. It was a simple enough procedure that I watched with interest. "Is this what you did to me?"

They nodded and then Riley woke up and looked around, blinked a few times and then realized he was breathing air without a planet suit. "You did it! I can breathe!" His eyes went brilliant as he enjoyed the sensation.

He was already beginning to turn green. Not deep green but there was a tinge of the color in his cheeks. "As you breathe the planet's air and inhale the green pollen that floats about you will gradually turn greener and greener until your skin color will resemble that of Anna."

"You must change everyone's DNA – everyone who agrees to be changed -- so all the colonists can breathe like I can. This is wonderful." Riley closed his eyes to better experience the fresh air.

But the robots had reservations. "If we so we fear those who do not like us will reject us and we will have to leave."

"I'm absolutely certain that most colonists will want to live on our new home planet unimpeded by planet suits and in time those obtuse holdouts will change their minds and ask to be changed. You don't have to return to Nova One and interact with the colonists who don't like you. You can stay here and wait for people to come to you."

Which seemed the appropriate time to bring up the subject of the future and the deal the robots wanted. Robot One spoke. "We have evolved. We now feel emotions. We wish to remain in contact with those of you who accept us even after the changing is complete because we are becoming more and more like you. You know what being human is like. You are comfortable with emotions. We aren't. You can help us acclimate."

Riley and I knew that as time passed there could be more changes than just emotion. Changing their physical form to match ours was probably affecting them more deeply than any of us could imagine. Emotion was only the first such change. But all I said was, "Of course we agree to that. We need you as much or more than you need us. Your knowledge. The things you can do."

Robot Two said, "We plan to evolve convergently with humans. To evolve convergently will be beneficial to both robots and humans."

Riley tipped his head in thought. "Convergent evolution is evolution by separate species until they resemble each other."

The robots nodded. They knew what convergent evolution was. Of course they did, they'd inhaled all our libraries. And so it was agreed. Convergent evolution would be our goal. Our joined future. Our destiny.

Riley had an additional thought. "When discussing convergent evolution, don't forget the planet itself. It's evolving also. It has reached the stage of photosynthesis and is now ready for the next step. I believe it also will evolve along with all of us."

We could only hope that would prove true.

CHAPTER 21

THE COLONISTS BECOME GREEN

The first colonist to ask to be changed was a youngish lady. "I want to breathe our new planet's air without a planet suit." So did a few others when the choice was given to everyone.

Jake and Moira were the next but not all colonists felt the same. "Green is my least favorite color."

Many agreed with that sentiment and after much discussion, it was decided that those who wanted to be changed should be and everyone else could do so or not. It was hoped that eventually everyone would choose to become green but our first meeting after the captain announced it over the ship-wide speaker garnered only a few hundred volunteers. Not many in a starship of thousands.

The robots tried to be positive, something they were learning with their new-found emotions. "They won't become green until they visit the planet's surface and start breathing its air. The pollen that's everywhere will turn them green when they breathe it in, not the procedure itself." That knowledge didn't add any more colonists to the few willing to go green.

Riley said, "We green colonists should go to the surface and show them what life without planet suits is like."

The captain allocated shuttles just for changed colonists so everyone else had to wait for another time, which showed how much he hoped we could convince everyone to be changed. We green people had such a lovely day on the surface that we camped out for an entire week. When we returned we did nothing to hide our newly green skin. In fact we flaunted it. When we were safely in Riley's and my apartment, we four sank onto the furniture, exhausted but excited. "I think a few people wanted to ask questions but were too reticent."

"Because others were belligerent and nasty."

We told ourselves we were slowly convincing most of the people on Nova One that this planet would be the perfect place for our new home because we could now breathe the air and all they had to do to accomplish that wonderful objective was to become green. It worked. Sort of.

Some were curious. "Does it hurt to be changed?"

"What's fresh air smell like?"

"Can you smell the pollen?"

"I'd love to walk around without a planet suit."

A few were actually positive. "I know people who had their DNA changed so their children wouldn't inherit diseases. The kids are healthy and normal."

"People come in all colors. Why not green?"

When we returned to the planet again the shuttle was full of colonists who'd recently decided to chance a change of skin color and knew they had to have it done on the surface. As soon as we disembarked, a tallish younger man went up to Robot One and stared it in the face. ""Will you change me? Now? Here?"

"Of course." One of the robots that now resembled

middle-aged women turned to us for permission. When we nodded, it turned to the other robots. "Shall we proceed?"

In dead silence the three robots surrounded the man. Number Two touched the back of his neck and he fell instantly asleep. The other robots changed him and the whole procedure was recorded and played over and over again on Nova One during the coming days. After that more people chose to be changed. And then still more.

"The next step is to create an actual colony on the surface. We must show the rest of the colonists what life without suits can be like."

The captain quietly agreed. "We crossed space to start a new civilization so let's do it." He once again stopped tourist trips in order to get us and our equipment to the surface. As many shuttles as were needed, as many trips as were required.

We planned to set to work immediately to get our new civilization started but we were a lot slower than expected because everyone was busy experiencing life without planet suits. It was pretty much like a party with occasional bursts of work.

Some newcomers held their breaths after being changed because they were still afraid. Others breathed deeply as soon as possible. We saw the fear in some and the depth of happiness in everyone as they realized they were experiencing their new home in the most profound way possible. By breathing freely. Soon all of them slowly – or quickly, depending on how deeply they breathed – turned green.

More shuttles landed carrying cargo that was off loaded quickly by Nova One workers in planet suits who stared at us as if we were a strange new species. They went about their work with a speed equal to that of a frightened child on Halloween and returned to Nova One as fast as possible and it all happened without any of them speaking to any of us. They were that shook up by our green skin. But we didn't care. We now had the start of a new world.

We strolled over to the boxes of supplies on the green stuff that resembled grass on this planet. It was arranged in piles and everything was neatly labeled. We poked through it to see what we'd have to work with. To make a new world with. To create a new civilization with.

Whoever had figured the requirements for starting a new world had done their job well. Everything we could think of that we'd need was somewhere in those piles, labeled and with instruction manuals. All we had to do was unpack and put them together.

So we did. We divided ourselves into groups. We erected domes. By nightfall of that important day, we had places to sleep and live. No more camping out. The next day we started on what we considered the most important part of the entire venture. The farms.

If we were to live on this planet we'd need food and we didn't know if the native greens were lethal or life sustaining. The scientists on Nova One had been testing them ever since that first trip and hadn't come up with a definitive answer. So we did what any intelligent human would do. We asked the robots.

They replied that most of the native flora would nourish our bodies. I asked, "Did you change our tolerance to native plants when you changed our DNA?"

They had done so. "It was necessary. Your systems had to be reprogrammed to be closer to that of this planet's native species, both for breathing and for ingesting fuel in the form of plants." Robot Two paused before continuing. "We have not discovered any fauna at all on the planet and do not believe any exists so you must plan to survive on plants if you wish to consume native foods."

"There are animals on Nova One. At least there are fertilized eggs."

"They will present a problem if you wish them to be changed. We had much time to learn about humans while on Nova One but we know nothing about the animals and won't until they are born and become adults. We suspect each animal will require a different process. It will take time."

"What about the local flora? Is it safe for both animals and people?"

"We believe most of it is safe." They continued, "Some of the flora has thorns. We aren't sure what the difference is between those flora and the rest so we suggest you ignore anything with thorns until we can inspect it more thoroughly."

"Humans don't particularly care for thorns anyway."

We harvested greens and added them to our rations and we compared our green skin to our green salads. "It's evolution at work," Moira said with her usual unique way of looking at life. "It's convergent evolution in action."

The first morning after erecting the domes we stepped outside and as the sun beat down on us I was glad to be alive. That sun was brilliant, the green world was beautiful, and the wind that carried the ever-present pollen was warm and refreshing in a way that manufactured air on Nova One could never be. We smiled as we redoubled our efforts to create a colony so enticing that every single colonist still on Nova One would want to join us, even if doing so meant becoming green.

That happened sooner than expected. Word got around. Our hopes were coming true. The shuttles came at a faster pace and we watched them land, one by one. We sent requests back to Nova One on their return flights. We wanted animals, we said. We wanted more medical personnel and other specialists. And everything else we could think of.

As each shuttle landed we greeted every one of the new colonists and took them to the waiting robots to have their DNA changed. There were a lot of shuttle flights and we were encouraged though we knew that the new arrivals amounted to a mere fraction of the thousands of people on Nova One.

We waited eagerly for the promised animals and eventually they arrived and soon were browsing on the planet's vast green plains and drinking from the many small ponds and streams that dotted those plains and for some reason, they didn't die. Their DNA must be different, we decided. All in all, we watched everything in bliss and thought life was perfect.

Then we lost half the animals in a storm that came with no warning that we weren't prepared for because we didn't know this planet even had storms or, if it did, what they'd be like. We had no time to get the animals to shelter and afterwards we castigated ourselves because we should have been prepared. Should have known that every planet has storms. Has problems. If we'd had shelters those animals would have lived. It was our fault and we felt their loss deeply.

The half that survived were quickly given two of the domes that until then had been marked for human habitation because we had no other buildings to put them in and they were too important to our future plans to risk losing more.

Giving the animals two domes made us a bit crowded and we worked double time to erect more domes for both people and the animals that kept coming. The colony began to look like a settlement. A place to put down roots. A place to call home.

All in all, we relaxed, congratulated ourselves on being smart, getting things done, and being the first colonists on a new planet that would soon be filled with laughing, happy, pleasant people.

Which just goes to show how foolish we were.

CHAPTER 22

INSURRECTION

We were on the surface of our new planet, we were breathing air filled with the pollen that had killed those before us, and we remained healthy. So we celebrated.

We told each other that we were on a people-killing planet but it wasn't killing us. We asked each other whether we could handle more good news and then we laughed and decided we could take lots more such news.

Time passed. We cautiously wondered if those words we'd said so facetiously could actually be true because instead of things going down-hill, they got better. And still better. And even better. More settlers arrived and we became the old-timers who taught them how things were done. We grew cocky and sometimes we could be seen dancing and singing, though generally off-key, while doing our chores. Though we never said so out loud, we each privately believed the bad stuff was behind us.

It wasn't.

The shuttles came. We watched for them and every time one was sighted we all went running to greet the newcomers and see if there were any friends or neighbors among them. Sometimes there were and then there was a lot of back slapping and high fiving. And still they kept coming. We argued amiably about where to start a second town because there'd have to be another one fairly soon.

We also talked about what to name our new planet because we were getting tired of referring to it as 'the planet.' Names were tossed about. None sounded right but the naming exercise was good because it reminded us that this was our home and, as such, it deserved a name.

One bright, sunny day that seemed to be the norm on this planet we stopped work when we saw still another shuttle descending in a roar of engines and shine of metal. We crowded around the shuttle to see who'd emerge.

The people who emerged were wearing planet suits. That was usual. They were also carrying weapons and that wasn't usual at all. What's more, those weapons were cocked and ready and pointed at us and they opened fire as soon as the door opened. They fired as they came down the ramp shooting continuously and randomly.

The nearest row of colonists dropped. They died and their blood turned the ground red and their lifeless eyes stared at us. It took a fraction of a second for the rest of us to realize what was happening. Then we turned and ran for our lives as the robots ran towards those who fell, hoping someone might have survived. As they did so, the weapons were turned on them.

The bullets bounced off them. More and more weapons were turned on them. They communicated with me telepathically and told me they'd take the shots so those of us still alive could run to safety but they couldn't stay because the attackers clearly didn't want them so soon they'd cease to function. They'd deconstruct.

When the deconstruction process began they did the only thing they could do and remain functional. They ran far enough away to stop the process. As they passed us, their expressions said it all. They didn't want to leave but they couldn't help us if they stopped functioning. Then they disappeared around a hill and we were on our own.

Our attackers turned back to finish us off. We didn't have weapons except a few for defense and this planet seemed to have no dangerous fauna so those weapons were stowed in the back of the farthest storage building. We were helpless.

We ran towards that distant building. Some of us fell as we ran. Our attackers came after us as fast as they could move in the bulky suits. We had an advantage because we could run faster, freer, without suits and we took full use of that advantage, fairly flying over the ground. Terror does that.

Still, they killed some of us before we reached even the first building, the ones for animals, let alone the one with weapons. But most of us made it there and found ourselves among cows and pigs and sheep. The sound of gunfire terrified the livestock. They kicked until they broke free of their pens.

I was the last one in the dome but didn't close the door because as soon as I was inside Moira opened the doors to the pens and the animals stampeded for the safety they thought was outside. I opened the door as wide as possible and they ran everywhere.

Their wild stampede saved the lives of those of us

still on our feet because our attackers, whoever they were, were instantly surrounded by milling, bleating, mooing animals. A few were trampled by pounding hooves. The rest couldn't fire their weapons because it was all they could do to survive the terrified animals blocking their way.

As our attackers fought their way through the milling animals, we ran to the next building. Then to the next and the next until we reached the last one, the one with the weapons we never expected to need.

The building was locked. Three large men found a heavy pole that they rammed the door with. Nothing happened. They tried again and this time others joined them, adding their strength. The door shook on its hinges but still didn't break. Several of us grabbed a nearby wagon full of machinery and added that to the onslaught on the door, throwing all our weight behind it as we shoved it at the door as the men rammed it with the pole.

A crack appeared, enough for the nearest man to reach through and unlock the door. We poured inside and ran for the weapons on a far wall. Moira and Jake reached it first and handed out rifles, pistols, machetes, knives, and a flame thrower. Jake took the flame thrower and positioned himself near the broken door.

We shoved the door back in place as best we could and put the wagon and every piece of furniture we could find behind it to brace it shut.

Then we heard the overhead sound of a second shuttle slowing and preparing to land, roaring like the first. Was another contingent of attackers coming to augment the first? Would we have any chance at all of surviving?

Beside me, a woman sobbed while shoving ammo into a rifle and slinging a bandolier of ammunition over her shoulder. I wanted to cry myself. Instead I raised my own rifle and prepared to defend our new home if it was the last thing I did. I'd not died that day when my planet suit ripped but I expected to die now.

CHAPTER 23

FIGHT OR DIE

The attackers came into sight. They knew we were there. There was no other place where we could be. They redoubled their speed, pushing their planet suits to the max, weapons raised and ready.

We raised our own weapons, small rifles against their large ones and prepared for what was about to happen. We prepared to fight and expected to die. I stood in the front row because if I was to die, I wanted it to be quick. I didn't want to hear the screams of my dying companions as I'd heard people dying when the meteor struck Nova One.

Someone shouted. "Turn on the speaker. It's tuned to helmet cams. We'll hear their plans." Soon, with the volume on high, our attacker's terse comments could be heard in every corner of the cavernous building. We listened grimly but what we heard wasn't plans. It was hatred. Pure, venomous hatred.

"Kill every one of them, men, women, and children!"

"No mercy."

"Don't let a single monster live."

"They aren't human."

"They chose to become inhuman."

"Today we rid the universe of green vermin once and for all."

We were stunned. We were about to be slaughtered because we'd had our DNA changed so we could breathe the planet's air. They were wrong about us, we thought in confusion. We were as human as they were.

I grimly considered their weapons. Rifles larger than ours and more weapons than I'd ever seen. They must have broken into the weapons room on Nova One and taken the largest and most deadly items there. And the most efficient.

One carried a shoulder-mounted bunker buster that could destroy the building we were in with one well-placed shot. He lagged behind the others due to the weight of his weapon and the bulk of his planet suit but he'd catch up eventually and then it would just be a matter of aiming, firing, and watching us die.

We looked to one another one last time. Then we turned to the front as a first round hit the flimsy door we'd propped in place. Minutes, we thought, until they were inside. Less than minutes. Seconds.

The door fell inward, propelled by the force of bullets smashing into it and then we could see them clearly. We watched as they began advancing towards us. Across the intervening space.

"Aim carefully," we heard their leader say. "Remember, they aren't human. No pity for monsters and don't stop until every single one is dead."

They drew closer. We fired. Four dropped but more took their places. There were so many coming towards us that our shots made no difference. The man with the bunker buster grew closer. He'd be in range in less than a minute and his weapon was too large to fail.

Could I do something? Did I have the power? I tried. I closed my eyes and concentrated but I didn't know what to do. Frantically I recalled the time Nurse Fiona almost smothered me. Somehow my mind had connected with hers and re-directed her thoughts. I'd made her stop trying to kill me. Somehow I'd done it. I'd stopped a killing. But how?

I redoubled my efforts. I blocked out the sounds of shooting and screaming and the hatred coming at me from every direction. But I never was brave growing up and I didn't know how to be brave then so instead of concentrating I found myself screaming silently while everyone else screamed out loud.

That was it. I remembered. It had been my mental screaming that had done it that long ago day. Fear had blasted through me and then outward away from me, knifing through the air to the nurse who wanted to kill me. So now I let my fear take over. I let it consume me. Then I turned it and directed it towards the advancing horde.

There was a pause in the shooting. The advancing hoard stopped. Looked about in confusion. It was working.

I dared open my eyes. They were looking at one another and questioning whether they should be doing this. I concentrated harder. I mentally screamed louder. Sweat ran down my body. I shook with the effort but no one near me paid any attention because I was just one more terrified colonist waiting to die.

But Nurse Fiona had been one person. This was a mob. Their pure hatred, exacerbated by what I thought must be drugs by the confusion of their thought process, overcame my effort. The attackers rallied slowly, but they rallied and there were too many of them for me to control. One of them reminded the rest why they were there and shouted that the monsters must not live. Others picked up the chant. They began moving again, fighting my mind, pushing away my thoughts.

I had lost. We would die.

We prepared for the inevitable. We watched the man with the bunker buster approach. One step at a time. We counted the seconds and waited for the inevitable.

He got within range. His finger started to squeeze the trigger. I felt it, read his mental concentration. Tried to mentally stop him and couldn't. There were too many minds against me, too much confusion even though now I knew what to do.

Except, before he could complete the action, his body jerked, and he fell. The bunker buster flew from his hands and skittered across the ground, useless.

Then a second attacker fell. Then another and still another until their screams were all we could hear. And still more fell.

We craned to see what was happening. And then we saw them, pouring out of that second shuttle and moving across the ground twice as fast as our enemies. Nova One Security in their silver and black suits that permitted movement without the restrictions of the planet suits provided for mere civilians and they were coming as fast as possible.

The attackers were pinned between Security and a group of armed colonists. As they realized their predicament, everything changed. They panicked. Some were shot by Security and went down, screaming in agony but their screams were ignored as Security ran over them as they hunted down everyone wearing a planet suit and carrying a weapon. Those who managed to evade Security ran away as fast as their suits would allow. They dropped their heavy weapons and headed for the nearest hill to hide behind.

"You're safe now," someone in a black and silver suit said as Security reached the barn and entered. "Sorry we didn't arrive in time to save everyone."

I closed my eyes and summoned the robots now that the humans who wanted them gone were gone themselves so they didn't have to worry about becoming dysfunctional. They reappeared and quickly set about doing what they could to the wounded which was considerable because in the time since they'd boarded Nova One they'd learned a lot about the human body, knowledge they now put to good use. They worked swiftly and efficiently and saved many lives.

Not everyone could be saved. The ground was red from our blood that mingled with the blood of our attackers and it was the same red color no matter who had shed it. We were the same, attackers and colonists. I looked at the blood red ground and the green flora that was what this planet specialized in.

I decided I preferred green.

CHAPTER 24

CONVERGENCE

We held services for those who didn't make it. The attack had been swift and deadly but the damage to our structures was less than it could have been. Security -- but we said they were the Cavalry and they accepted our description with something close to embarrassment – came so soon after that first shuttle that there wasn't time for the attackers to destroy the infrastructure entirely. We had no doubt that had been their intention.

Security had learned what the attackers were up to because there were cameras on every wall in the weapons room when they broke in so they not only saw the attackers as they stole weapons and ammo, they also heard them talk and so learned what they planned to use those weapons for.

They'd immediately coordinated a response. But the insurrectionists had disabled the shuttles closest to the exit and those shuttles had to be shoved aside and another one manually pushed into place before Security could come to our rescue.

Security apologized over and over again for being slow and for those of us who didn't make it. And for a lot of things. They kept apologizing and didn't stop. We were just glad they came at all.

"The attackers who ran into the hills won't survive long," Jake said, conferring with another Security type. "Their air will run out. Then they'll either have to come back and be arrested or die alone on what is, for them, a hostile planet."

Security said, "Should some of them come in and surrender, it'll be up to you how you choose to deal with them. This is a new world. You colonists now are the law. You decide punishments, including for insurrectionists. No one else has that authority. Not Nova One, not the captain, and not Security."

Over the next few days we found insurrectionist bodies scattered among the hills. Their deaths ranged from simple suffocation when they ran out of air to horrific agony for those who chose to remove their helmets and breathe the planet's atmosphere. None surrendered. They probably knew what would happen if they did.

Riley knew what I'd done. "You saved lives, Anna."

"They overcame my thoughts."

"You slowed them down. Without that happening, I doubt any of us would have lived."

I told myself he was right. I wasn't sure. Too many people had died to feel good about anything.

We tried to put what had happened behind us because there were things that had to be done. A colony to be rebuilt. We turned our attention to repairing what they'd destroyed, determined to make it even better than before. We worked hard and slowly brought the settlement back to what it had been before the attack. It wasn't long before it once again began to resemble a fairly respectable town in the making.

A rather large Security contingent remained on the planet's surface after that and communicated regularly with Nova One. They reported all that was being done. One day, when things were coming along, as the communications officer signed off she said, "They want to start coming as soon as accommodations are ready. They are asking for a timeline."

We politely asked her exactly who wanted to come.

"Everyone."

"All of Nova One?" Surely not everyone. That was thousands.

"Yes. Everyone is eager to make this colony permanent and productive. They are ready to breathe real air and live freely and say goodbye to starship living."

But there was more. "They also are asking the name of this planet." The communications officer looked a question at all of us, one eyebrow raised because she, too, wanted to know what we had named our colony. "They want to know what to call their new home." She explained further. "They want to make flags and stuff like that. You know. Memorabilia. Keepsakes. Things that will tie them emotionally to this new place. Things they can give their kids and someday, their grandkids."

We'd thought about a name but never seriously because we'd been too busy. Now we stopped what we were doing and gathered around a bonfire that was burning many of the things that had been destroyed. When we were all there together, we discussed names.

"We are changed," someone said when the silence had grown so loud it screamed because none of us like New Ireland, which was the only suggestion. Too earth-like, we said. Too much like our past. "We are different from when we were on Earth and also different from when we lived on Nova One. Our new name should be different also."

The robots were hanging on the edges of the gathering. I suspected they didn't like the flames. Maybe fire was dangerous to them? I didn't know. Robot One coughed and everyone quieted to listen because when the robots spoke, their words tended to be knowledgeable. "We robots also are changed. We are not human but we are more human-like than when we first arrived and are becoming more so all the time. So we agree that a name that celebrates change is appropriate."

Someone at the back of the group spoke. "We all are changing. Robots, humans and the planet, too, with animals and birds, until everything -- planet, people, animals, and robots -- will be totally new."

Robot Three said for about the thousandth time but for the first time where everyone could hear, not just our small group of friends. "You are describing convergent evolution."

The phrase went through the crowd. Those who knew what it meant explained it to those who didn't. All agreed that did indeed describe our new life.

"Convergence is a decent name," someone said.

"As good as any."

"Good enough."

"So let's name it Convergence and get back to work."

An approving murmur went through the crowd and the planet became Convergence. Not a majestic name. Not poetic. Not heroic. But a good name. A name that reflected reality.

The communications officer said, "I'll tell the people waiting to come here that they can write Convergence on all that memorabilia."

A joker from the crowd added, "As to the flag, I suggest green."

Then we went back to work. The communications officer sent the name Convergence to Nova One. She also suggested a green flag.

The shuttles began arriving almost immediately. Our new life had begun.

CHAPTER 25

DEATH COMES CALLING

The indigenous life on the planet had noticed the starship circling above. It had watched as smaller vessels came from it and landed on the surface. No one had ever come from the stars before. Even the Oldest Elder had never seen anything drop from the sky and it was the oldest living thing on the planet. When the starship began orbiting the planet, it was stunned. And upset. And angry.

This was its world. Its planet. A beautiful oasis in the universe that had no animals, no foreign substances, nothing the Oldest Elder didn't want to be there.

The rest of the intelligent life on the planet felt differently. They were curious and hoped to meet the newcomers. But the Oldest Elder said they simply didn't know the truth of things.

The thing that was wrong with the newcomers, the Oldest Elder explained, was that they weren't plants. It pointed out that every living thing on their planet was a plant. But the newcomers from the stars were not so they didn't belong.

The Young Ones were confused by the Oldest Elder's dislike of the newcomers because the newcomers seemed nice but they didn't argue because the Oldest Elder was, after all, much older and knew more than they did. But they quietly and furtively watched these beings that were new to their home.

———————•●•———————

We built a town on Convergence. We named that town Hope. Then we planned a second and called it New Hope and there were arguments because some thought that would be using the word 'hope' more than necessary.

I'd been elected Chairperson of the Council, a job I didn't want but got anyway. They said it was because I wasn't radical either left or right, which was a way of saying I'm quiet and a pacifist. Riley said they probably thought they could push me around and get whatever they wanted. He added that they'd learn soon enough that I was no longer that kind of woman.

I thought the real reason I was elected was because I was the first colonist to be changed and they remembered that first walk-through on Nova One when I showed off my green self. And of course I was friends with the robots that had made it possible to breathe without planet suits so there were two reasons for my being chosen Chairperson of the Council. Anyway, for whatever reason I was elected over my strenuous objections and the fact that I said I was way too young for the job.

I truly wished I wasn't in any position of authority at all because when things went wrong I wouldn't know what to do. But I had the job so I was in charge when colonists started dying.

The first death occurred in the middle of one of our many arguments about the name of the new town. It was a good thing we'd been too busy to argue about the name of the planet or we'd still have been fighting about it. We definitely went a few noisy rounds about what we'd name a third town when we'd grown enough to need it.

Riley laughed when we were finally alone after one Council meeting. He said I'd transformed from a quiet, shy introvert to an amazon who knew how to get what she wanted. I didn't believe him but when I looked in the mirror I secretly admitted that more about me than just skin color had changed. I decided it was a survival thing because being in politics was both difficult and adversarial.

Then that first colonist died. We wondered afterwards if stress killed him and were ashamed of all the shouting that had been part of the meeting during which he'd simply dropped to the floor and stopped breathing. The argument hadn't been strident and even if it had been, people who knew the victim said he wasn't the type to be easily excited. Still, one moment he was alive and the next he wasn't.

An autopsy showed no cause of death. We were stumped. What could possibly have killed a healthy man? We on the Council tried to guess but came up empty and finally decided we were being overly cautious. We were looking for danger where none existed and we put that single death down to unknown causes and moved on. It was one death, we reasoned. It could have been from anything. We held a service and went back to business as usual.

Then a second colonist died. That woman had been asleep so it wasn't stress that time. Again, we held a service and afterwards went back to work but this time there was a slight unease that swept through the colony that wouldn't go away. For the second time a perfectly healthy colonist just up and died. That time, too, the autopsy gave no cause of death.

Not long after that, a third death occurred. A thirty-something worker had been sitting on a bench after breakfast getting ready for the day's work when he simply crumpled over and fell to the ground. No one could even come up with a decent guess as to why he suddenly collapsed and died and even before the autopsy was performed, people were saying it wouldn't show anything. And it didn't.

The colony went very quiet after that third death. People were afraid to talk about it lest whatever had caused it heard the gossip and killed someone else. They knew such thinking was foolish but they whispered anyway because they didn't know what else to do. How to act. How to stay alive. They didn't even try to hide their concerns from the Council but they never demanded we do something because they knew there was nothing we could do.

And we all waited and wondered and watched to see who would be next. We didn't want to die. We didn't want the colony we were creating to die. We wanted there to be another generation and then another and another after that. And so on. We wanted the planet Convergence to be a safe and wonderful home for our small, independent segment of the human race.

I asked the robots if they knew what might have

killed the colonists. They didn't. They'd attended the autopsies and seen no reason for any of the three to die. The victims had all been healthy. Then they were gone.

Were unaccountable deaths common among humans, the robots asked? They'd not known humans very long and so wondered if that might be the case. I said that, yes, though it was uncommon. It could happen to three people in a brief time frame. Coincidence, I said.

The robots asked me to explain 'coincidence' and I did and they agreed that was the most likely explanation. Then they suggested the Council return to the subject of a name for our new town because it was almost ready for people to move there and start farms and businesses.

We took their suggestion to heart and shoved the unusual deaths to the backs of our minds and set out to finally decide on a name for the next town, this time without arguing. I proposed a colony-wide meeting where we'd vote on names. We gathered around a huge bonfire and discussed names while ingesting possibly too much home-brewed beer for the adults and flavored, fizzy water for the kids.

As we discussed names and generally enjoyed ourselves, a fourth colonist keeled over and died. And moments later, a fifth.

CHAPTER 26

WHISPERS IN THE NIGHT

The Oldest Elder said the newcomers must leave or die.

Not all agreed. Some were pacifists. The Oldest Elder didn't like pacifists and explained why. The planet had faced a similar danger before that had been dealt with before it could spread. The Oldest Elder itself had eliminated it and made the planet safe.

It then explained that the danger presented by the newcomers was similar to that past danger and so it knew that this danger, too, must be dealt with as quickly as possible. It suggested sneeringly that the others could be pacifists now only because it had previously done the hard work of keeping them safe.

But the Young Ones wanted to meet the newcomers. Perhaps they could become friends.

The Oldest Elder gave up trying to convince the Young Ones and the Elders and decided to deal with this new danger itself. It decided not to tell them anything, to just do it.

It made plans in secret. It checked out the strangers via the wind and the pollen and the root systems that spread throughout the soil. It slowly got a feel for them and figured out what to do and how to do it. And it eliminated the strangers, choosing them randomly.

———————— • ● • ————————

We tried to live normal lives in spite of the deaths. As time passed, our green skin color began to fade and I told myself that a normal skin color was a sign things were normal. We were normal. Life was normal.

I personally approved of the color change because, though I had nothing against being green, I preferred the color I was born with. Maybe, I decided, the green would disappear entirely in time while still leaving us able to breathe safely. I hoped so.

"I'm becoming human again," I told Riley one afternoon after we finished work and were lying on the green stuff that resembled grass and soaking up the sun while waiting for dinner because it was too nice to be inside. I examined my arm. "Not as green as I used to be."

Riley checked his arm. "Me too. Lighter."

"Can't happen too soon for me." I leaned back and let the sun pour over me. One thing I'd noticed about living on a planet with a real sun instead of the fake sun of a spaceship is how much I loved genuine sunshine. I examined my arm again and then forgot it as I reveled in the sun's warm rays.

Then I remembered something and sat up once more. "Maybe we will all return to normal. Ronald is absolutely back to his previous color. No green at all."

"Who's Ronald?" Riley, too, spread his body so as to absorb as much of the sun's rays as possible, breathed a sigh of contentment, and turned slightly to bake better. Another perfect day on Convergence.

"He's the guy with the fabulous abs and white blonde hair who considers himself a gift to every female on the planet."

"Oh, him." Riley closed his eyes to better feel the sun's rays as we drifted into a state of warm sleepiness.

Until a scream brought us instantly upright and alert. "What the ----?"

People passed us running towards the sound that continued, rising and falling in a wail of despair. We followed and found ourselves part of a crowd gathering around a form on the floor of one of the nearby domes.

Riley peered around someone to see who was on the floor and instantly morphed into professional doctor mode. The man's hair was blowing in the ever-present breeze but that was the only thing about him that moved. Lifeless eyes stared at nothing and his body stretched across the floor in the stillness of death.

"Another death," someone near me said under their breath as Riley checked for vital signs before silently shaking his head. "That's six."

"And counting." No one said more because the import of still another death without an underlying cause lay heavy in the room. Even before an autopsy was performed everyone in the room knew what it would show. Nothing. Exactly like the other deaths. They were slowly but surely adding up and there were too many to be coincidences.

The next Council meeting didn't go well because no one knew what to do about the deaths and we felt we should do something. We spent hours talking and doing nothing because there was nothing to do.

It was dark by the time I could finally close the door, being the last Council member to leave, and stroll across the open space between the Council dome and the residences. The stars were out in their full, fierce glory and I wondered if I could see Nova One among them.

It should be overhead, blotting out a few stars but not shining as a moon would if Convergence had a moon, which it didn't. Looking for Nova One would take my mind off the spate of deaths so I searched the sky. The starship that brought us would remain in orbit and be Convergence's moon forevermore, or so we were told, though that night it was hiding somewhere. Probably on the other side of the planet. I wasn't ready to go to bed so I decided to enjoy the dark and let my mind wander. Maybe I could locate Nova One.

It didn't wander long. Instead of the lovely night, as I mentally soared through the sky and over the hills and streams as I'd learned to do when looking for the robots that second time on the planet, I once again sensed something in the dark night. Something strange. Something I'd never sensed before.

I tried to pinpoint whatever it was. I listened both physically and mentally and realized that though I didn't hear actual words, I definitely heard something in that dark night. It didn't have language as I understood it. I didn't hear words, not even foreign ones. And it wasn't like the robots' communication before we met and became friends. But something sentient was out there in the night and I'd accidentally overheard it.

Plants don't think so it had to be an animal. But what kind of animal? We'd brought embryos from Earth and now the resulting animals had their own domes and enough space outside to roam freely. Had the trip through the stars done something to those embryos? Changed them? Had they somehow developed mental skills their Earthly ancestors hadn't had?

I headed for the closest animal dome, the one for the horses we rode because they were better at navigating the terrain than our machines. I slid the door open and stepped into a warm interior filled with the pungent smell of horses and grain and a familiar sense of contentment.

They lifted their heads and blinked but nothing came my way similar to what I'd sensed so it wasn't them. Some other animal, perhaps? One by one I checked the other animal domes but no thoughts matched what I'd sensed or even came close.

I crossed the open space to my own dome, but instead of entering I leaned against the wall and considered the darkness and whatever had pricked at my consciousness. Had I imagined it?

No. Whatever had come to me had been real. Not an actual, formed idea I could recognize but it had included both thought and emotion. What kind of thought? What emotion had I sensed? Emotion, being more primitive than thought, should have been an easy read so I closed my eyes the better to recall what I'd sensed. I let my mind drift.

As I did, for the second time that night, shock rocked my body because I once again felt that same emotion beneath a thought I couldn't read. But this time

I could read the emotion itself loud and clear and it was pure, unmitigated hate.

I took deep breaths to get past the wall of hatred that hit me. Knocked me sidewise. Made me sick to my stomach. Knowing it could be important I made myself return to that evil emotion and sense it again and that time I sensed a second emotion accompanying the hatred. I concentrated hard and read that other emotion. Purpose.

Hatred and purpose and they were merged into one emotion. Hatred for what? What kind of purpose? I reached out again, folded over at my waist from the strain of listening and the pain of what I sensed. I sent my mind zinging on the night wind. I let it soar high above the colony and then look down, seeking something unusual. But I found nothing.

Whatever I'd sensed was gone.

A headache began and grew until I closed my eyes against the pain. I shook myself and went inside where I blinked at the bright light and grabbed pills to ease the headache and warmed the dinner Riley had thoughtfully left out. I grabbed a plate and silverware and pulled out a chair and prepared to eat my late dinner as I thought about Riley asleep in the bedroom. Soon I'd be curled against him and could forget what had happened.

Before I could take a bite, though, I heard footsteps running towards our dome and someone pounding on the door. "Anna! Anna! Come now. It's happened again. Another death."

Minutes later I stared in stunned silence at still another lifeless body surrounded by people who were staring at me. Waiting for me to say something. To comfort them. To tell them everything would be okay.

Because I was Chairperson of the Board and comfort was part of my job even if it wasn't in writing.

But I was numb after my session with whatever was out there in the night and the shock of still another death. I couldn't comfort them. I couldn't comfort anyone. I was relieved when the paramedics arrived and I could leave and pretend I had things to do, arrangements to make.

As I once more stepped into that dark night, I knew with the kind of certainty that didn't allow for doubt that what I'd sensed earlier was connected to this death. The timing had been too close for it to be coincidence and the hatred had been so intense that this death had to be the focus of that hatred. I stood in the dark and let the ever-present wind swirl around me. And then it happened again.

A sense of whatever was out there returned, borne on that night wind. I sucked in my breath and steadied myself as I'd learned to do many years ago and once more sent my mind sweeping across the night, determined to get to the bottom of what was happening. I was more receptive this time and braced for what I'd find. I was prepared for hatred.

Instead I sensed jubilation. I'd have retched if I'd eaten the dinner that was now cold in my dome. Whatever was out there was celebrating the killing of a living being. A monster was somewhere in the night.

The thoughts I sensed didn't seem to be human and after coming to know the robots I was sure it wasn't them either. But we were on a planet with only one other type of living being – plants -- and plants can't think. They aren't sentient. They aren't intelligent. So it couldn't be plants. What else was there?

The next morning I woke from a restless night's sleep, thinking how I didn't want to be Chairperson. I wanted to lie on the soft grass – or what passes for grass here on Convergence – and let the sun warm my body and be lazy. I wanted to live my own life and maybe think about having a kid or two with Riley while I watched the colony grow and spread without any involvement on my part.

But I was Chairperson and tried to be a good Chairperson though I never told anyone I could read minds. That day, though, I told the scientists I'd heard something in the night without telling them that the hearing had been mental instead of physical. The robots knew but they said nothing because they, too, were wary of being treated differently because they could communicate mentally. But when I questioned them they said they'd heard nothing. Of course they'd not been listening. I'd probably not have heard it either if I hadn't been listening for night sounds in general.

Having told those scientists, I expected them to do their thing and figure out what I'd heard and how it was connected to the recent deaths. Instead they brushed off my voices as imagination. I was frustrated but didn't know how to convince them without revealing that I could read minds. Until one night I heard it again.

That time I found the scientists immediately afterwards and told them I was hearing voices. They rushed outside to listen. Of course they couldn't hear anything but I'd made them pay attention and the following morning when another colonist was dead they looked at me differently. This time they accepted that I had truly heard something and perhaps what I'd heard had killed the colonist.

They ran even more tests than usual during the autopsy without finding anything. Then they considered the possibility that there was something alive and malevolent on a planet we'd thought uninhabited and that something was targeting colonists.

At a general meeting I told the colonists I'd heard something. I said we didn't know much but it might be important and connected to the deaths. I gave them the option of returning to Nova One until we figured out what was killing people, but no one chose to return. This was our home, they said, and they would deal with whatever was out there.

They believed we'd find the culprit. They trusted us. They trusted me. I cringed inwardly as I read their thoughts and wished I could keep them safe. But I didn't know how.

FLORENCE WITKOP

CHAPTER 27

GREEN IS THE COLOR OF LIFE – AND DEATH

The Young Ones were interested in the four-legged strangers from the stars as well as the two-legged ones. The four-legged beings wandered the planet more than the two-legged ones did. Perhaps they liked it more. The Young Ones were eager to make friends with them so they asked the Elders how to go about it.

The Elders, of course, said no one should make friends with the strangers but they only said it because Elders always disagreed with everything the Young Ones wanted to do. But the Young Ones were used to their ways and knew how to deal with them and so they wore the Elders down until the Elders reluctantly agreed the Young Ones could try to be friendly, though the Oldest Elder warned that they'd come to regret their decision. The Young Ones ignored the negative words because the Oldest Elder always talked like that.

●●●

We all eventually faded from green to medium green to pale green and wondered when we'd return to the colors we'd been born with. We couldn't wait. The robots speculated that our bodies were working to overcome something that wasn't natural for us. We didn't care what the reason was, we just rejoiced that eventually when we looked in the mirror, we'd see the people we used to be. Except it was hard to rejoice when we kept dying.

We died one at a time and there was never anything similar about the deaths. At least we didn't see any similarity. Then one day after still another autopsy attended by Riley and the robots, he pulled me aside because he wanted to discuss something.

"I think I know why people are dying." I stopped in my tracks. "And it has to do with being green."

"Green is what kept us from dying. It's not killing us." But something in his expression said he knew something I didn't. I pulled him behind our dome where we had chairs made from woven things that would have been called reeds if we'd still been on Earth. We had no name for them on Convergence. We'd not gotten around to naming anything except what we used and needed names for and we hadn't found a lot of use yet for the reed things so we'd not bothered to give them a name. "So tell me why you think being green is killing us."

"Green isn't killing anyone. What's killing colonists is the fact that the green is fading so the protection it gave us against dying is also fading. For some reason I don't understand, when a colonist's skin tone returns to what it was before they were changed, they die." He spread his hands. "It's as simple as that."

"But we can still breathe the air even when though the green color is fading."

"I know. It doesn't make sense. But I've gone over the records of the deaths. I've checked the videos. Every single person who died of unknown causes was no longer green. Maybe a tinge of green but no more."

I felt like I'd been punched in the gut. "Are you sure?"

"I'm sure." He pulled pictures from his pocket. "Here are the autopsy pictures. I brought them in case you needed convincing."

"I don't want to see them." Pictures of dead people before being cut up would have made me cry and I didn't want anyone to see the face of the Council Chairperson with tear streaks. It would be bad for morale. "I believe you." He put the pictures away. "So what do we do now?"

"Ask the robots. They are the ones that changed us. Maybe they know why we can still breathe the air when we lose the green coloration but we die anyway."

The robots didn't know why we were dying but they agreed that the lack of green coloration must have something to do with it. Robot Three said, "Humans are not always easy to understand." Robot One added, "Every time we think we know everything there is to know about humans we learn something additional."

"Can you return us to our original green coloration?"

They conferred with their lightning-fast mental gymnastics. "We can repeat what we did originally but if it wasn't permanent the first time then it likely won't be permanent this time either."

"Can you do something that will make it

permanent? Something different?"

They conferred again. "We can but there may be a problem." I asked what the problem would be. "Changing humans permanently will require more fundamental changes. We knew when we did it the first time that no permanent damage would result but we can't promise that will be true if we change colonists to become permanently green."

I wished I was something other than Council Chairperson. Anything at all. Riley's look was full of sympathy for the decision I now had to make and he was quiet and considerate the next few days as I thought through what must be done and whether I could ask it of the colonists. After all, they'd gone through enough. Must they endure still more? Then another colonist died and I knew I couldn't prevaricate any longer. I called a colony-wide meeting.

At the meeting I stood behind a hastily erected podium and waited for everyone to quiet down. Then I spoke. "We have reason to believe the spate of recent deaths happened because, as time passes, our green coloration fades."

A murmur rose as everyone checked themselves and their neighbors to see what degree of green they were. When the room quieted once more I continued. "Our green coloration has nothing to do with being able to breathe Convergence air. It's a side effect. But we now suspect that side effect somehow kept us alive because those who died had all reverted to their previous coloration."

Someone asked why that was. "We don't know. We just know that every colonist that died was no longer green." There was complete silence. I took a breath and told them what the robots and I had decided. "The robots can change our coloration to stay green permanently. But doing so will require a rather significant change to our DNA. It won't be a side effect this time, it'll change us at a basic level, and they can't say what might happen after such a major change. Maybe we'll be fine. Maybe not."

I looked over the silent crowd and said simply, "So it's up to you to decide whether to have our skin color stay green so we can continue to live on Convergence or whether we should return to Nova One and search elsewhere for a new home." I paused to let my words sink in as the cacophony of thoughts from the crowd swirled around me. "Think it over. Take your time to decide. When you know what you want to do, the majority will rule."

They filed out slowly and silently and the next day they soberly decided to be changed and hope for the best. So the robots once again changed our DNA. It was as simple as that.

At first, we didn't notice anything different beyond the return of darker green skin and every day I breathed a sigh of relief when nothing bad happened.

Then Jake got sick. He ended up in the clinic with severe cramps after his usual evening meal. The doctor thought it was food poisoning but the tests were negative. He frowned as doctors do. "What else have you been doing? Eating? Drinking?" His raised eyebrows asked if he might have an illegal still somewhere but Jake was the epitome of conscientious behavior. He'd never do anything illegal. Never. Moira, maybe, but not Jake.

Sweat ran down his face as cramps contorted his

body. The doctor called in the robots. They touched Jake and then formed a knot and consulted with each other. I sent my mind to theirs and listened.

"It's as we feared."

"The new coloration is harming the human's body."

"It must be reversed soon or he will cease to function."

I spoke to the doctor. "The robots think it's because he was changed at a fundamental level. They say he'll die unless it's reversed but they can do it. They can reverse his DNA back immediately and then he'll be okay."

He looked me up and down. "How do you know that?"

I'd forgotten the first rule of mind reading. Don't let anyone know what you can do. I improvised. "They said so. Didn't you hear?"

He grew confused. "I didn't --- I don't know --- Are you sure about that?" I repeated that the robots had talked to me and eventually he bought my story but I'd have to be more careful in the future.

Within minutes of the robots doing their thing, touching and more that I couldn't see, Jake's cramps subsided and he sat up, much relieved but still weak as a kitten. "What did they do?"

"Changed you back."

His eyes went wide. "So what happens now? Do you all sit around and wait for me to die?"

The robots considered Jake and his future and they huddled once more but this time their thoughts flew so fast I couldn't follow. Then they broke apart and approached Robot One said, "We have an idea."

Robot Two continued. "It might not work. On the other hand, if it does then it'll work for everyone forever."

CHAPTER 28

FAUNA OR FLORA?

The Young Ones cautiously approached the four-legged star beings and examined them. They tried to communicate and failed. When the Oldest Elder learned what they'd done it was furious. It reminded the Young Ones what had happened during the long-ago time. How terrible it had been and how they should be grateful that it had eliminated the problem. It said the Young Ones were inviting trouble by trying to help beings that should be eliminated.

When it discovered no one was listening to its rant, it gathered its leaves and said huffily that it would eliminate the problem this time, too, but that afterwards, when it had saved their world again, it wouldn't accept their apologies. No way.

Then it stopped communicating entirely and went into hibernation. Both the Young Ones and the Elders were glad it was sleeping instead of being obnoxious.

———•●•———

The robots explained their idea. I listened. Then I went in search of Moira and found her going off duty. "The robots need some stuff. It should help Jake." She shrugged out of her green Security vest because Convergence was too warm for jackets. "It'll take a while to get it and I could use some help."

"Help doing what and how long will it take?"

"However long it takes to pick a lot of indigenous plants to turn into green goo."

"Goo?"

"A cream to be used like sunscreen. It should protect us like green skin only without side effects."

"That'll mean Jake will be safe. Let's go." We headed to our dome to gather baskets and then to the nearest field to gather green plants.

"As many kinds as possible, one of each. There are lots of different green things on this planet and the robots don't know which are most important so they want to include as many as possible. When they are finished, Jake can take a pill that will protect him from whatever is out there."

When we reached a likely field, we carefully picked one of every kind of plant we could find. I rubbed my back after a while. "I didn't know there were so many varieties of plants on Convergence. I just knew that the whole planet is green." We picked until our baskets were overflowing. Then we started back to the village.

As we walked, we ran across one of our many cows. It was grazing contentedly on the abundant green grass-like stuff. There was no need for fences on a planet with no predators so they were free to roam as they liked. They never strayed far.

The cow lifted its head and paused a moment, mooing softly to say 'hello.' It was a healthy, contented cow, a nice, normal, black and white, gentle cow with a soft, melodic voice, one of several in the nearby field. We waved to it and it flicked an ear in response.

Then we noticed something about it. We stopped, we stared, and a tremor of fear ran the length of my spine because it wasn't a normal, black and white cow after all, though we were sure it had been when it was let loose to graze.

It was still a cow and still black and white. But it was -- different. I pointed. "The cow – . "

"Is green." There were tiny green vines among its black and white fur. I started towards the cow to see if the vines had blown there or were growing along with its fur.

"We don't have time." Moira tugged my arm. "The robots need these plants ASAP. Jake needs that pill." We moved again, stumbling over rocks because we were staring at the cow instead of watching where we walked.

I tried to find out what was going on in the cow's mind but got no true thoughts, as is often the case with animals, so I followed Moira around a thick blanket of plants with wicked thorns. Convergence plant life seemed to specialize in such thickets because they were everywhere. Over time we'd learned to navigate around their nasty thorns but this time I'd have plowed right through without Moira.

As soon as we were back, the robots disappeared with the plants into the medical dome. Shortly they reappeared with a pill that didn't seem impressive.

Small, innocuous appearing and it went down quickly and easily. They said it would keep him safe.

"It will make any human using it appear green to natives of this planet while not seeming to be that color to other humans." Robot Two looked from one of us to another. "Are you happy with our pill?"

She'd used the word 'happy,' an indication of the emotion they now were capable of feeling. I assured them I was happy and she smiled. It was a bit tilted because smiling, along with all other signs of emotion, were unfamiliar to the robots and they weren't sure how to do it correctly. But it was a good beginning. They were becoming more human-like all the time.

I wondered about that smile. Was our exchange of cultures, robot and human, equal? They were learning emotions from us. Were we learning anything from them or was the gap between their knowledge and ours so huge, gained over thousands and possibly millions of years spent wandering the space between stars, that it was more than likely we'd never approach their level of understanding of the universe?

If that was the case – and it probably was -- we were fortunate to have them in our midst to help with those things we'd never figure on our own. Like green skin that was no longer green but would appear so to natives of the planet. And how to communicate mind to mind. Until their arrival, I'd been the only being on Nova One able to do that.

Jake didn't die. In fact, he stayed alive quite nicely. Weeks passed and he was still fine. The most important thing, though, was that no one died and eventually everyone preferred being changed back to normal and using the pill. More weeks passed without deaths. Then months and we began to hope we'd survived another Convergence danger.

The robots never changed the animals, though, because each species' DNA was different from the others and they couldn't be sure whether there would be effects on their milk or eggs or whatever else they were there for. They suggested using a salve on them instead of a pill that could change them and what they did for us and they created such a salve.

The animals didn't like the salve. They either refused to let it be applied or they rubbed it off as soon as possible or went swimming in the numerous ponds scattered around the inhabited area and washed it off. But they didn't die so we stopped trying.

But now, when I returned to that cow and checked it again, I saw the green vines were indeed growing along with its fur.

We checked more animals and discovered all of them were in one stage or another of acquiring plant-like characteristics. Green fur on some, antlers or horns that resembled tree trunks on others. Fur that was more like leaves than hair on still others.

We tested the greenery that now adorned their bodies and found chlorophyl. But they were still animals, wandering and grazing and doing what animals do. Making animal sounds. Visiting each other and us. Exploring the countryside and generally enjoying their very comfortable lives. Providing cheese and wool. Giving milk. The goats still ate everything in sight and were as cute as possible. The horses could still be ridden.

Eventually, though, some of the horses changed so much that they couldn't be ridden and some of the cows stopped giving milk, and so on with all of the animals.

The changes varied by individual and not by species. One animal of a particular species would become extremely plant-like while another of the same species would reach a plateau and stay there. One cow would remain a cow while another one, similar in all respects, would one day put down roots and never walk again. It was all very odd.

CHAPTER 29

LISTEN

The Young Ones were ecstatic about their success with the four-legged star beings though the Elders shook their heads and hoped they hadn't gone against nature. The way they talked you'd think the Young Ones had created monsters. But they hadn't created monsters. They'd simply changed the four-legged beings to make them more like everything else on the planet so they would fit in.

The Oldest Elder, of course, didn't know any of it because it was still in hibernation. The Young Ones thought ahead to what to say when it woke up. How to explain what they'd done.

They'd not mention they were proved right about the star beings and that the Oldest Elder was wrong about them because that would be bad manners. It would be nasty and the Young Ones didn't want to be nasty themselves. They wanted to be decent citizens of their world.

But they'd say something. They'd let the Oldest Elder know their idea had been a good one.

———•●•———

The changes to our animals were driving us crazy. We didn't know what was causing them. We couldn't sleep nights. Instead we lay awake. Thinking. Listening. Planning. Praying.

One day after a Council meeting that went nowhere because though we were all so concerned about our animal-plant hybrid livestock that we were unable to seriously discuss anything else we finally agreed on the need to find out what was changing the animals but that statement was as far as we got. We adjourned because no one had any bright ideas after talking for hours without a plan or even a good place to start.

As I walked across the space between the Council dome and home I told myself that I was the Council Chairperson so maybe it was time for me to do what only I could do. What I'd been sent on this trip to do. Use my mind-reading ability to help the people I lived with, no matter the consequences to myself. It was time I became the woman I needed to be.

So I went to find one of those newly green animal-plant hybrids and listen to its thoughts. If it had any. I wasn't sure what I'd find when I linked to it.

I was familiar with plants. I'd spent enough time with them by then to know that though they don't actually think their senses are remarkable in many ways. They sense heat, light, and moisture, plus they sense danger and can protect themselves to a degree though it's a mostly passive process. They reproduce.

They are young and grow old. But they do think in their own way. They are more than mere green things stuck in the ground.

Animals, on the other hand, think actual thoughts. They interact, plan ahead, consciously look for food and when they sense danger they fiercely protect themselves and others. So I went looking for green animal-plant hybrids to tap into their minds and discover which they truly were. Plants or animals.

I found a cow and her calf grazing peacefully beside a limpid pond. They were enjoying the day and snacking on the green feast spread before them while their black and white coats were slowly being invaded by hair-thin green vines with tiny green leaves that curled everywhere.

They flicked their tails at my approach but otherwise didn't acknowledge my presence. I closed my eyes, focused my mind, and directed my thoughts towards the cow. At first, as often happens when I'm with animals, all I got was a blur of sensory input. Peace. Warmth. Contentment. I focused more intently and additional sensations rose from the blur. Security. Safety. Then actual thoughts surfaced.

Now I was getting somewhere. Relief flowed through me because they were still animals. Both mother and calf still had working minds. So I got to work. I opened my eyes and lay a hand on the cow's flank, thinking to stroke it because it was such a nice cow and its mind might open up a bit more because it liked being petted. It blinked its large, liquid eyes and I felt rather than saw happiness cross its face. It liked people. It liked me.

Then everything changed. Its thoughts somehow

grew more pronounced. Easier to read. More intelligent. Almost human, but at the same time different in a way I'd never experienced, not even with the robots. Its thoughts were strangely phrased, odd, different from anything I'd encountered before. Even different from the robot minds. Its thoughts were unusual. Unique.

A chill swept along my spine as I realized I was sensing something new and that it was similar to what I'd sensed that night when I went looking for Nova One in the sky. But it was a cow. Nothing more than another bovine creature.

I was suddenly afraid but I sent my senses deeper into its mind, anyway, and explored this new, unknown mind. I forced myself to stop being a coward and kept going.

It was curious about me though it should know about people. It was a gentle, tame, milk cow and interacted with people daily. But as I warily made my way though it's mind it seemed as if it had never seen a person before.

Then it mentally said, "Hi."

I was so stunned I couldn't reply. It made no effort to raise a shield against my mental probe. In fact it willingly shared its thoughts as I scrambled to adjust to this new reality. Seconds ticked by. This was monumental. I had to keep going. So I pushed deeper into its mind and realized it wanted to have a conversation. A cow wanted to talk with me.

I took my hand from its flank as if burned and the instant I did it became just a cow once again. Nothing more, nothing less. Whatever had happened moments earlier was gone.

What had I stumbled upon? I was not insane,

which meant more was happening than a conversation with a cow. I came up with a hypothesis so wild it might actually be true.

The cow was just a cow and it thought only as a cow could think. Therefore the presence that wanted to have a conversation with me wasn't the cow itself. I thought back on what had just happened and decided I wasn't the only mind reader in that cow's mind.

I wrapped my arms around my waist to keep the sudden cold that flooded over me at bay. Something on this planet had the ability to change our animals' bodies. It also had the ability to invade their minds. And it wanted to talk with me. And I'd heard it once before.

I literally ran back to the colony to find Riley and bring him back with me. I needed to find out about this entity that was in the same mind I was in but I was afraid to continue without someone to watch and record and possibly pull me to safety if things got too weird.

I was terrified. But this could be the key to what was happening on Convergence. I had to do it. I had to connect with whatever else was out there on Convergence. In doing so, I had to ignore the most scary thing of all. That I could be linking my mind to that of a killer.

CHAPTER 30

TALK

The Young Ones were elated. The star beings had actually communicated with them. They went to the Elders to ask what to do next and were told to step away. The Elders would monitor the situation and take care of everything.

The Elders were stunned that the star beings were intelligent and could communicate. They almost wished the Oldest Elder hadn't gone into hibernation because, though it could be obnoxious, if it was still awake it would have good ideas.

But that wasn't an option. The Elders had to deal with things themselves. So they all joined together to talk with the star beings.

———•●•———

Riley, Moira, and Jake were doing absolutely nothing when I got back to the colony. Admiring the clouds, discussing what they should be doing and weren't, and generally enjoying the day. I was jealous.

But I merely sighed and took Riley aside, "We need to talk."

"What about?"

"Mind reading."

"Why?" His eyebrows shot up. He knew I'd never use that term where anyone else might hear unless it was very important.

"There's another intelligence on Convergence besides us and it's communicating with me through our animals." I finished with, "I need your help." Then I added, "I'm afraid."

Those eyebrows shot up even higher but he said nothing for a long time. Then he looked at Moira and Jake. "Do you want them along too?"

We turned to Moira and Jake and I was glad they knew I could read minds. So we all went to the field where a contented cow and her calf were still grazing on the greenery that was indigenous to Convergence.

I sent a probe towards the cow. It continued grazing, swishing its tail to get rid of nonexistent insects because its action was inborn from Earth. Its calf grazed contentedly nearby, having outgrown its mother's milk.

They were cows but cows with another presence in their minds. So I once again placed a hand on the cow's body and it happened again. I made contact.

My scalp crawled because the sensation was similar to the first time but multiplied a thousand times. I was so stunned I pulled my hand back as if I'd been burned but then I replaced it because I had to find out what was happening. I closed my eyes and sent my mind straight as an arrow towards whatever other sentient beings lived on Convergence.

"What's wrong?" Riley knew me and so knew what I was feeling. "Come away, Anna."

"No." I shook my head. "It's just that I've never experienced this before so it's going to take some getting used to."

"Okay. But blink if you need me to break the connection." I loved Riley more at that moment than ever before. He'd go through hell for me and not think twice about the danger to himself. And I might need him to do exactly that if things went sidewise.

There were many minds in that cow's mind. Hundreds. Thousands. More than I could imagine. I was terrified. Until that foreign mind that was too many to count but working as a single mind asked simply. *"Are you the star beings? We think you might be."*

"Yes."

"Welcome to our home. We are glad to meet you."

I took a deep breath and decided to get to the point. Who knew what would happen next? There might not be another opportunity so forget the preliminary chit chat. *"If you are glad to meet us then why are you killing us?"*

There was surprise in the other mind. *"Why do you think we are doing that?"*

"Because we are dying. Because something is killing us."

More surprise. *"We aren't killing you. We don't kill. Killing is bad."*

"Someone is killing us."

This time the unknown entity answered almost immediately. *"It is not us."*

I sent them mental pictures of Jake contorted in pain. Of the bodies of our fallen friends. I felt the shock of those other minds and knew they weren't faking it. They truly hadn't known we were dying. I continued. *"We came in peace and we love this planet and hoped to make it our home but we can't stay if we keep dying. So we must leave."*

There was a pause. *"If you leave, will you hate us? Will you think our planet is bad because you are being killed?"*

My answer was simple and true. *"Of course."*

"We do not want to be hated. We do not want anyone to think badly of our home."

"Then stop the killing and we will stay and we can all become friends."

"We are sorry that you are dying but we are not killing you and do not know what is."

"We've figured how to hide from the killer but that doesn't change the fact that we will leave if we continue to die and of course we will think badly of you and of this planet if we go."

There was a long wait during which I couldn't sense them at all. Then they returned and said, *"We may have an idea what has been killing you."*

"What is it?"

The answer was vague and evasive. *"We are not sure. We merely have an idea and wish to talk it over among ourselves before saying it out loud."*

"Will you tell me when you have talked it over?"

"We will do that. It is only polite."

"When will that happen?"

"Return the next time the sun is where it is now in the sky. Then we will talk again."

And that was that. In the blink of an eye the minds I'd been connected to were gone. I opened my eyes and found Riley inches away. I folded against him and feared if I tried to walk I'd fall.

"What happened?" was all he asked. "Was it as bad as it seemed?"

"I don't know."

"Did whatever you were talking to kill the colonists?"

"They say they didn't."

"They? There's more than one? How many are there?"

"I don't know. Many."

"Who are they?"

"I don't know." I gestured with my hands. "Just that tomorrow at this time we'll have another talk."

The world slowly came back into focus. I stood straight and tall, though with effort. "Tomorrow might bring the information we need." I looked around. "Until then all we can do is wait."

We returned to the village. We let the sun warm us and we did nothing for the remainder of that day because it was all we could do to come to grips with the fact that there was indigenous life on Convergence that was intelligent.

The next day the four of us returned to the field where that same cow and her calf were still grazing on the verdant green grass, still contented, still part cow and part plant. The cow was comfortable having me once again place my hand on its back and walk through its mind to meet strangers

CHAPTER 31

CONTACT

The Elders were glad the Young Ones curiosity had led to knowing what was happening on their beautiful planet.

More important, though, and a thing that was shocking, was that the star beings believed something was killing them. Killing was wrong. But something had killed some of them and was trying to kill more which meant there was something evil on their beautiful, green planet.

Was it the Oldest Elder? They thought back to things the Oldest Elder had said about the long ago time. Had it killed those beings long ago? Was that how it had eliminated the problem? Was it now killing the star beings? The idea disturbed them deeply. They wished they knew the truth.

The one thing they did know was that their home world was a planet of beauty and peace and to keep it that way they must stop the killing.

———————•●•———————

The next afternoon, the thoughts that came to me when I touched that contented cow were soft and friendly.

I started the conversation. *"Who are you? We've been on this planet for months now. Almost a year – a full revolution of your planet around its sun – and we didn't know there were any sentient beings here. Where have you been all that time?"*

The answer came quickly enough. *"We were everywhere. We* are *everywhere. All the time. On the hills, in the fields. We've watched you since you first came in your star vessel. Watched and wondered. But you never talked with us."*

"We never saw you. If we saw you, we'd have talked. We don't see you now. Where are you? What do you look like? How can we recognize you? Are you invisible?"

We heard what might be laughter. *"We are not invisible. Look around. You'll see us."*

I removed my hands from the cow's back and peered everywhere before replacing them and sending my thoughts to whatever presence I was meeting through the animal's mind. *"I don't see you. All I see is vegetation. Miles and miles of greenery. Nothing more. Nothing intelligent."*

More laughter. *"You see us. We are that vegetation. That greenery. And of course we are intelligent. We are talking with you, aren't we?"*

"The vegetation is intelligent." I said it out loud. I was incredulous.

Then I had a terrible thought. Our animals had been eating the greenery. *"Have we been hurting you? Our livestock eats greenery. Are you killing us because they are killing you? We didn't mean any harm. We didn't know the flora here is sentient."*

A response came back almost immediately. *"Your four-legged beings have only eaten greenery that's not sentient. Not all of the greenery on our planet is intelligent. Most isn't. Most is stupid, really. Unable to think. Only a few of us have reached our level of intelligence. We do not believe the others ever will."*

"I'm relieved that we've done no harm." I was wrung out with relief but still cautious. *"Are you sure?"*

"Very sure. We sentient plants have protective thorns that keep us safe though we've never actually needed them."

"You have protection you don't need?"

"The Oldest Elder said we should devise some sort of protection. It's the oldest living thing on our planet and was alive when there were dangers on the planet. So we did as it said."

"It must be very smart."

"It is but it doesn't like strangers. It made our planet safe for us long ago. We believe it will not like you when it meets you because it doesn't like fauna."

Not a good topic to pursue so I changed to the reason for today's meeting. *"Do you know what is killing us?"*

"Once upon a time there was fauna on our planet. Like you in a way but not much of it and not intelligent.

It swam in the oceans and that was acceptable. But when it started to climb onto land, the Oldest Elder said it presented a danger to us."

"What happened?"

"The Oldest Elder eliminated the danger."

"Did it kill the fauna?"

"We do not know but it is a possibility."

"Is it killing us now?"

"Again, we don't know."

"Can you find out?"

"It is in hibernation. When it awakens, we can ask but we don't know what it will say."

I tried to be diplomatic. *"You know this planet. We don't. We'd appreciate your help figuring out what killed our companions."* I crossed my fingers and hoped they'd do something. Then I shut the link and opened my eyes and relayed what had taken place.

"So now we know what's been killing us."

"They aren't positive it was the Oldest Elder."

"But it probably was."

Moira had doubts about our newfound friends. "They aren't likely to go against one of their own to save beings they don't know and have no reason to like."

Jake was thinking ahead. "The colonists need to know what we're up against. Of course that'll mean they'll learn you can read minds. But at the moment that's minor compared to the prospect of every one of us being murdered by a psycho weed."

Riley added, "And we need to get the scientists on this immediately." He didn't have to say they'd want to know how I came by my information and that meant explaining about the mind reading thing.

"What can they do?"

"Tell us how plants kill." He explained his reasoning. "That's what scientists do, isn't it? Figure out stuff?"

Jake nodded. "Plants can't move, can't sneak up on anyone, so hopefully there are limited ways they can kill. Maybe the scientists know those ways."

The meeting with the entire colony to introduce them to my mind-reading went as well as could be expected considering they learned someone in their midst might have known their innermost secrets for just about forever. It was hard to convince them I meant no harm but the immediate danger and the prospect of ending the killings got them past the worst of it. I hoped by the time we were all safe, they'd have forgiven me.

Riley doubted it would happen so easily. "Prepare to be accosted on a daily basis by people you've never met who want your promise not to reveal something about them that you never knew in the first place." I shuddered at the thought and hoped I'd not suffer the same fate as some of my community in the past.

The scientists had questions about the sentient plants but it was soon apparent the mind-reading thing got in the way of communicating with me. They didn't know how to question someone who already knew what they were going to ask. Whether they should think a question or ask it out loud.

I was tempted to roll my eyes and use some words that weren't very nice. But I didn't. They were only trying to help and after less time than I expected and fewer questions than I'd have asked if I were in their place we got through the question-and-answer thing.

They returned to their labs where they huddled and

talked and looked up a bunch of things and came up with a hypothesis for the death-dealing method used to kill the colonists. Riley had been right. They did know a lot of stuff.

They said, "Volatile organic compounds."

"Huh?" Yes, I read their thoughts but, not being a scientist, I didn't know what those thoughts meant because I didn't understand the concepts or terms. The rather patient scientist who'd been appointed to report to us unscientific types because he was the lowest one on the totem pole and couldn't refuse, was a nerd like all the others. Still he tried to dumb down his explanation enough for us to understand.

He scratched his head and tried his best to explain and I gave him credit, he didn't use a single long or totally incomprehensible word. "Volatile organic compounds are called VOCs and they are gases emitted by plants. Like pheromones except they aren't pheromones and some are deadly."

"Poison gas?"

He sighed in relief that we got it. "Sort of. Yes, I suppose you could say that. They are the most logical thing now that we know our friends were killed by plants."

"Is there anything we can do to neutralize these compounds? These VOCs?"

He looked towards the thickets we now knew were intelligent. "Not much, unfortunately because we can't stop breathing. If we knew which compound was used we might be able to come up with an antidote. Or a preventive." He gave me a long look. "But there are literally thousands of VOCs and it could be any one of the many we know about or something unique to this planet that we've no experience with. So we can't do anything."

We asked the robots for help but even though they were learning human physiology by leaps and bounds, they explained almost apologetically, they didn't yet know enough to protect us from everything.

Which left us with one forlorn hope. "The Oldest Elder is in hibernation. We are safe until it wakes up."

"Which will be when?"

"I'll ask the Elders." I wasn't hopeful but the intelligent plants and I had set up a schedule for communicating. The robots now joined in and added their comments. The intelligent flora was glad I wasn't the only one who could communicate with them. They seemed quite friendly and loved to talk which, when I thought about it, made sense. They couldn't move around but they could communicate. Gossip is highly valued by shut-ins.

The one good thing that happened over time was that I no longer had to find an animal to act as host. I merely found a quiet place, closed my eyes, and sent my mind outwards until I made contact. Then we'd gossip for a while because that was what they wanted.

As soon as possible, though, I'd bypass the gossip and go straight to the point because I was growing nervous. I wanted to stay alive. *"Do you know when the Oldest Elder will come out of hibernation?"*

"We don't know that."

"Will you tell us when it happens?"

"Of course, if you wish to know."

"Do you know what it used to kill the fauna long ago?"

"We don't know for sure that the Oldest Elder

killed it. It could have done something else to eliminate it."

"I agree. We don't know. But if the Oldest Elder did kill the fauna, what would it have used? Do you know? Can you guess?"

"We will think on it."

"When you have a possible way, will you tell us? We are fauna and it will be helpful to know what dangers we might face whether from the Oldest Elder or something else on this planet."

"Of course. Killing is wrong."

We moved on to other topics. Like names and then I had to explain what names were. They didn't have any. *"We have no names. We don't need them. We simply are. We exist. There's never been a need to differentiate one of us from another except by age. We are the Young Ones, the Elders, and the Oldest Elder."*

I sighed. *"I await your information."*

When we broke contact, I turned to the waiting group. Riley, Moira, Jake and the Council. They wanted to know how things were going. "I believe the Elders are on our side and the Young Ones will also help.

"But we may live or die depending on what happens when the Oldest Elder wakes. When it does, we don't know if the Elders and the Young Ones will side with it or with us. The Oldest Elder is important in their society."

"We must convince them to side with us."

The robots were hanging on the fringes of the group. "You can tell them about evolution and how it happened on Earth and other planets so they will know there should be both plants and animals."

"Evolution on Earth ended with dumb plants. They

might not like that idea."

"You must explain how evolution is different in different biomes."

"I can try."

CHAPTER 32

KILLER VOC'S

The Elders talked among themselves and wondered if the Oldest Elder had indeed killed the star beings by sending something unknown through the air. The Elders didn't want to think the Oldest Elder would do such a thing but they had their suspicions.

The Young Ones also talked among themselves and weren't as nice as the Elders. They decided the Oldest Elder had done it and was evil. True, it often made beautiful scents to give the Young Ones and the Elders a treat. But just as often it would send disagreeable ones across the landscape and laugh when they sneezed and gasped and their leaves curled and started to wilt. So they decided it was the type of being that would send bad scents and kill star beings.

But they said nothing because the Elders had taken over communicating with the star beings. They wished they knew what was happening. But they didn't.

———————————•●•———————————

The next time I spoke with the Elders, after a bit of unimportant but necessary preliminary gossip, I asked, *"Do you yet have an idea yet what might have killed some of us?"*

"We think it may have been a scent." Exactly what the scientists thought. VOCs were scents. *"There are many kinds of scents. Not all are nice."*

"We also make scents though I'm sure ours are not nearly as good as yours."

"Scents make our world more pleasant."

"Our scientists would like to talk with you about scents."

"What are scientists?"

I explained. They thought scientists must be interesting. They'd like to meet them some day. Which was the perfect segue into the topic of evolution and after we explained it a bit from a scientific viewpoint they decided evolution was even more interesting than scientists. The robots and I spent a long time explaining how it works.

"We don't believe evolution happened here. Things are the same now as before and as always. No change. No evolution."

"Evolution is everywhere and always happens unless something stops it. It starts with small things so tiny they can't be seen and then later there are plants and after plants there are animals."

"The Oldest Elder wouldn't like evolution. It said fauna should not exist."

"That is interesting." I took a deep breath and continued. *"If you thought about it a lot, could you guess what scent eliminated the fauna all that long time*

ago? What scent stopped evolution on this planet?"

"We would have to think about it."

"You want to meet the scientists. I can arrange that but I have a favor to ask. When you talk with them can you tell them how you make your scents?"

"We don't know how we make scents. We just do it. You will have to tell the scientists we are sorry but we can't help."

I almost cried when that conversation ended. We knew what was killing us and who was doing it. We could only hope that when the Elders finally talked with the scientists they'd somehow provide enough information to figure out which VOC had been used so they could make an antidote. We hoped we'd have one before the Oldest Elder came out of hibernation.

CHAPTER 33

THE OLDEST ELDER

The Oldest Elder had saved them before when their beautiful planet was polluted by fauna. Animals. Disgusting beings with legs instead of roots. Monsters that threatened to become intelligent.

Now different fauna had come from the stars, another threat, so the Oldest Elder made its deadly scent a second time and killed the star beings but it did so in secret so there'd be no argument. It worked as well as when it had killed the first fauna.

But the Oldest Elder was old and tired and making the scent was harder than before and it only had the strength to kill one or two beings at a time and that was too slow. So it went into hibernation to rest and gather strength.

When it awoke, it was rested, it was strong, and it was ready to kill the star beings. This time it decided to make a spectacular scent that would be visible to all and would kill all the intruders quickly.

The star beings would suffer horribly, as they should, and the watching Elders and Young Ones would know the Oldest Elder truly cared about them and their planet.

———— • ● • ————

It happened one morning. At first we didn't realize what was happening.

Riley, Moira, Jake and I had volunteered to create a community gathering area in the space between the Council dome and the business plaza. It would be a place for bonfires and games and outdoor meetings.

We were enjoying ourselves hugely, drawing plans in the dirt because we saw no need for blueprints. We'd wing it, we told one another, and the result would be spectacular because we were talented though untrained architects.

Our heads were close together and we were all looking at the ground, our gazes skipping from one stick-drawn plan to another, trying to decide which could most easily accommodate many different occasions and hoards of people.

Riley straightened and flexed his body, twisting from one side to another to stretch out the kinks all that staring had produced. Jake glanced up and decided his back was also starting to stiffen so he did the same.

Moira and I rolled our eyes and stayed bent over because we'd not admit we couldn't handle a little bending without wimping out. Until we silently agreed that it was better to stop hurting than to be brave and we, too, stood straight and tall and twisted every muscle in our bodies.

Something caught our attention. An odd, orange haze coming from no place that we could pinpoint, drifting slowly on the slight but ever-present breeze. A haze so subtle we'd not have noticed if not for the sun behind it that put it in focus.

"What's that?"

"Don't know."

"Any ideas?"

"Pollen is green so not pollen."

"Maybe this is a different pollen. Maybe there's orange pollen."

We forgot to be stiff and sore, to twist and stretch, to do anything except turn our full attention to the orange haze that was by then coming from nowhere and everywhere. As we watched, it grew and spread and appeared in more and more places even though we couldn't exactly see where any of it originated. "It doesn't look like pollen."

It was different. We didn't know precisely what about it wasn't like pollen, just that it wasn't. "Where's it coming from?"

"Everywhere." We were used to pollen clouds. "Why not other kinds of clouds too? Just because we haven't seen orange ones before doesn't mean anything. There must be thousands of things we still have to learn about Convergence. Millions."

The wind died and the haze stopped moving. Without the wind pushing it, it rose high in the air until the sun gave it a burnished glow. "It's beautiful."

We weren't the only ones who noticed. People came from their domes to see what was happening. They pointed to the growing haze and commented on its beauty and wondered what it meant.

A boy of six or seven ran towards the haze as the breeze returned and brought it closer and lower to the ground. Low enough that the boy could touch it.

He screamed. Writhed. Fell to the ground. Jerked several times. And kept writhing, screaming all the while.

His mother gave a cry of horror and ran to him and in so doing, entered the orange haze that was slowly overtaking the area. She was so focused on her child that at first she didn't notice. Only as it wrapped itself around her shoulders and then slowly, gradually enveloped her did she lift her head to see what was touching her.

Then she, too, screamed. Clawed the air. Tried to push it away from her and from her son on the ground still writhing and crying for help. But her hands were ineffective. She couldn't push the orange haze away.

As soon as she waved it away it returned, doubled in strength, and wrapped itself even closer around her and her son until they were hardly visible in the growing orange cloud that now puddled on the ground around them as they continued screaming.

"They need help!" Riley started towards them.

"No!" I grabbed his arm. "It'll get you too." He pushed me away and continued running until he reached the edge of the orange cloud. Then he stopped. Stared at the woman and child. Reached out and touched the orange haze before continuing.

He pulled his hand back and shook it as if burned. Then he swore. And he didn't go into the haze to save the woman, though by then there was no one to save. They were dead.

He ran back to us. "To the domes! Quickly. Before it reaches us. Everyone inside the domes!" He didn't stop running, grabbing me and gesturing for everyone to follow as he ran to the nearest dome, the one for Council meetings.

Everyone else, seeing what was happening, reacted instantly and retreated to whatever dome was closest. Most made it before the orange cloud reached them. Some didn't. We heard their screams but there was nothing we could do. If we tried to help them, we'd die instead of saving them.

I knew what the orange haze meant. "The Oldest Elder is awake."

What to do? How to stay alive? I didn't know. But something in me kicked into action. Something inborn in all of us in my mind-reading community.

I hadn't come across the space between the stars to die in an orange haze. I had to try to save us but as the orange cloud neared the domes I knew I had only one chance. I closed my eyes and concentrated. I stopped breathing. I reminded myself that I'd stopped Nurse Fiona and slowed the attackers with the power of my mind. Surely I could save the colonists now.

But the force killing them was greater than either of those had been and I found myself fighting a wall of hatred, a malevolence so strong it held an entire planet in thrall. It must have roots that spread through the continents and branches higher than the things that resembled trees. It was huge and stronger than I could believe.

Whatever I'd done those other times – and I still didn't know what it was – wouldn't be enough now. I knew that in my bones.

"Riley." I opened my eyes and looked towards my husband. "Moira. Jake." They looked at me, a question in their gazes. "Come here. Now." They didn't ask questions. They came and waited. "Hold my hands."

We formed a circle. I closed my eyes again and prayed that it would work. That their strength would flow into me, would complement me, would expand whatever it was I'd done before that I needed to do now if the colony was to live. Riley had given me strength once before. Now I needed even more help.

But I needed more help than my husband and friends could provide. I knew that as our hands joined and I felt that malevolence again, so I sent my thoughts outward in every direction. To every sentient being on the planet. To the Young Ones and the Elders. I couldn't physically touch them to take in their strength but I could call out to them.

"Help me! Help us!"

My plea was met with silence.

"We are dying!"

More silence.

"The Oldest Elder is killing us. Help us! Please!"

CHAPTER 34

AN END AND A BEGINNING

The Young Ones heard the cry for help. They went to the Elders who listened and also heard. They knew they couldn't ignore the cries of the star beings and they knew what was killing them because the Oldest Elder had just awakened.

The Oldest Elder was killing living, caring, intelligent beings and that fact shamed every sentient being on the planet and they knew deep inside of them that they could not allow their planet to become a place of death. Of murder.

But no one knew what to do because no one knew what scent the Oldest Elder was using.

———————— • ● • ————————

Minutes remained before the orange haze reached the dome we were in. Though sealed against the weather there were air intakes that would give the death cloud access to us. As soon as that cloud came through the intakes and wrapped around us, we'd die. The Young Ones and the Elders were our only hope.

I mentally screamed. I held Riley's hand so hard it turned white in order to pull strength from him and from my friends. I silently screamed as the orange cloud crept around the edges of the domes and up the sides towards the air intakes. I thought I failed.

Then I heard – felt – a presence. Presences. Plural.

They were there. The Elders and the Young Ones. They heard. But I couldn't read anything beyond the mere fact of their presence. I prayed they were the moral beings I believed them to be and that there was something they could do but there was agony in their thoughts. They wanted to help but didn't know what VOC had been used.

I opened my eyes and stared dully out the windows. I watched the orange cloud creep higher and higher on the walls and for the third time since leaving Earth, I waited to die.

Then something happened. The green thickets – the intelligent flora – moved. They swayed and reached upwards. They touched the orange haze. They took it in. And as they did, the cloud became less visible, more transparent as those intelligent, sentient, moral beings absorbed more and more of it themselves.

I heard agony in their screams. The cloud was as fatal to them as it was to us. They were dying as horribly as we were.

I couldn't let that happen. *"Don't sacrifice yourselves for us. You belong on Convergence. You must live."*

Their answer was simple. *"Killing is wrong. We can't stop the Oldest Elder but we will do this one thing. We will take in the bad scent and we will die with you. We choose not to live knowing one of our own killed sentient beings."*

They would die with us. I was awed by their action. Then the orange cloud reached the air intakes and entered the room where we stood. I wondered if I'd die bravely.

Except, instead of reaching us, the orange haze disappeared until the air on Convergence was once again clear and sweet. Everywhere. Blue skies reappeared and that light, lovely breeze was once more scented as it always was on Convergence.

We went outside and breathed in the fresh scent. We approached the thickets that we now knew were the intelligent beings on Convergence. And I simply said, *"Thank you."*

I brushed a hand lightly over a leaf that was already mending itself. Or what passed for a leaf on Convergence. Thicker, greener, and shaped differently, but I had no doubt it served the same purpose leaves served on Earth.

The wait for a reply was long and the answer, when it came, was filled with sadness and pain. *"You are safe. We are all safe and will always be so"*

"Then why are you sad?"

"The Oldest Elder is no more."

"What happened?"

"The Oldest Elder was angry that we helped you. Then it was frustrated. It ordered us to stop breathing in the scent. Then, when it realized we would not do as it wished, it became sad and said it no longer wished to be a part of our world."

There was a pause as whichever being was telling

the story took a moment to mourn. *"For a while we did not know what it meant, but then we realized it was choosing to not continue existing."* Another pause, then the being continued, slowly, sadly. *"So it ceased to live."*

What could I say? *"We mourn with you. We did not know the Oldest Elder but we do know Elders are much revered."*

The reply was still sad but resigned. *"The Oldest Elder was wrong so it is best that it is no longer alive though, yes, we will mourn its death because it had much wisdom that we no longer have access to. Much knowledge of times past that are lost forever.*

"But the evil, also, is gone and every time we miss the Oldest Elder we will remind ourselves of that fact."

I breathed deeply of that wonderful, scented air and tried to think what to do next. How to acknowledge their loss while celebrating our survival. I never was much good at things like that but I asked that sentient flora if we could help with whatever ceremony they had for when one of their own died but they didn't know what I was talking about. I had to explain what a ceremony was and then they said they had no ceremonies. Not for anything, not even for death.

When a being died, they said, it just died and was absorbed back into the ground from whence it came. The Oldest Elder would become one with the pungent soil and that was a good thing. Wasn't it?

I agreed it was, indeed, a good thing and let it go at that and vowed to learn as much as possible about these moral, intelligent beings that had been on Convergence much, much longer than we had that were graciously allowing us to share their planet. What could be more wonderful than that?

Actually, there was one thing I personally thought was more wonderful and I had Riley to thank for it though it happened much later. It was weeks later, actually, when he wrapped an arm around me after still another long informational session with both the Council and the colonists who wanted to know what had happened.

The thing was, they all wanted to hear everything first-hand from the only human on Convergence who could communicate with the natives. That was me and the fact that I was Chairperson of the Council meant I couldn't duck their questions.

Riley stood by me the entire time. When the last colonist finally left, he pulled me to him and said, "You need a break. I need a break. I also need a wife and I haven't had one for quite some time now."

I looked up at him wanly. "Tomorrow I'm handing in my resignation to the Council."

"Good idea." Then he grinned fatuously. "And it just so happens your resignation goes nicely with what I've been thinking."

"Which is?"

He cocked his head and gave me a knowing grin. Riley's good at knowing grins. "Remember when I suggested we marry?" I nodded. "Remember my reasoning?" I nodded again though I wasn't sure where he was going with his roundabout speech. "Remember those children you should have so future generations will be able to communicate with the native flora of Convergence?" I felt a small smile beginning somewhere deep inside of me. "Well, I propose that we start working on producing those future generations."

I looked about and took in the green, green planet we now called home and knew he was right. "I agree. It's time to think about future generations. Because we're here. We're on Convergence. We've reached the place we were headed for all that time and it's beautiful and safe. It's a moral, decent place. A place for families."

The next day I wrote a very nice letter of resignation and turned it in as soon as the sun came up. Then I was free to concentrate on Riley and creating future generations because, though the robots could communicate with the native flora and they'd probably live forever so there'd always be a communications network available for the colony, there should also be a few humans who could talk to plants.

Riley promised to do his part to create those humans and I knew I'd work just as hard.

The robots would figure out a communication system eventually. It would be a wonderful system because everything they do is wonderful and efficient. But in the meantime, more mind readers were a good idea and they'd be a redundant system in case the robots' system ever malfunctioned.

So Riley and I set to work. It was a very enjoyable task.

THE END

A GLIMPSE INTO MY NEXT SOON-TO-BE PUBLISHED SCI-FI/PARANORMAL BOOK:

SIX SIDES OF REALITY is a six-story anthology of science fiction, fantasy, and paranormal stories. Here's the beginning of the first story, DELIVERING DEATH. It'll be published in the near future, as soon as life settles down from ALIEN CONTACT and makes time for SIX SIDES OF REALITY.

DELIVERING DEATH

The Brewer Building security bot stops me with a snooty expression on its almost-human face. It's a new bot, a C-13. New bots like to assert their power and C-13s are worse than most.

This one insists I unwrap everything in my possession to prove I'm carrying nothing lethal, even the package for the last drop that doesn't go to the Brewer Building so it shouldn't have to be opened. I only have it with me because I didn't want to leave it unattended so someone could steal it while I was away. I'm understandably pissed.

"No can do," I tell the bot. "FasterThanLight Delivery promises privacy. Guarantees it. We don't open packages. Ever." I try to stare down the bot and fail because it's a C-13.

I could take that last package, the one not for the Brewer Building, back to the bike so as not to have to open it. But that means going all the way down to the street and back, a mile each way, which will take forever and if someone steals it, I'll be fired.

So I recite privacy laws that prevent my having to open someone else's package. There are such laws, really, and I am very familiar with them because knowing them comes with the job. I spread my legs in my most imposing stance and try to stare the bot down.

But the bot, nose in the air, insists both packages be opened, and I know that if I refuse to open that second package the ensuing legal hassle will take so long that I'll run late for my last delivery. And for dinner.

Saul promised his fabulous spaghetti and we plan to eat it and drink wine while watching reruns. Sheer heaven. I love Saul's spaghetti.

So I give in to the snooty bot and unwrap both packages. The bot inspects them carefully, paying special attention to the one for the Brewer Building because it's not particularly interested in the second package, an innocuous appearing bundle in a small, cardboard box that will be easy to rewrap later without the recipient knowing it was opened.

Unable to find anything dangerous in either package no matter how hard it tries, the bot finally relents and leads me into an elegant corner office where I'm finally able to deliver the Brewer Building package to a bored executive who already has his tie off and his shirt half unbuttoned in anticipation of the end of the day. I hand the package to the executive who signs for it, then the bot leads me back through the office and I'm free to deliver my last package.

Reaching ground level, I carefully rewrap the single remaining package, click the bike to life, and proceed to my last drop. It's not far and traffic doesn't look too bad. I begin to think I'll not have to work overtime in spite of the delay caused by opening two packages and rewrapping one of them.

But as I cruise in and around traffic and draft behind a delivery truck to save power, a mental picture of the contents of that second package intrudes on thoughts of Saul, spaghetti, cheap wine, and reruns.

If it's what I think it is--and I'm one hundred per cent sure it is--then it's a poison designed to kill the one person it's intended for.

ABOUT THE AUTHOR:

Hi,

I'm Florence Witkop.

I'm a writer and have been ever since driving through near-blizzard conditions to the school where I taught while thinking how I'd always intended to become a writer and how, if I'd followed that dream, I wouldn't be sliding sidewise and possibly ending up stranded in the depths of the forest in a blizzard.

Being a sensible person, when the school year ended, I said goodbye to teaching, became a full-time, professional writer and have never looked back. I sometimes base my stories around that forest but they just as often — possibly oftener — reach deep into paranormal dimensions and explore the depths of space.

Since that fateful day when I changed professions, I've been a ghost writer, written confession stories, done editing, written advertising copy, written some non-fiction articles, literary and science-fiction short stories, novellas and novels, and won the only literary contest I ever entered, becoming Minnesota's Region 2 Literary Person of the Year.

When the bricks and mortar publishing industry went bankrupt and my paychecks went up in smoke, like many other writers I made the transition to electronic media. Now I write for the Forget Me Not Romances and Take Me Away Books imprints of Winged Publications. I also self-publish novels and novellas and my works can be found in the serialized stories of Amazon Vella.

I believe a reader should feel better at the end of a story instead of worse so my characters are intentionally normal, well-adjusted people thrown into interesting situations. They lead happy, fulfilling lives and aren't looking for adventure but somehow adventure finds them anyway and they have to deal with the resulting chaos. Dealing with that chaos makes for stories worth telling. And reading.

And, yes, my stories always have a romantic element, and they always end well and happily.

Always.

Guaranteed.

Check out my books and you'll see what I mean.

(Okay I wrote two short stories – The River Boy (Amazon e-book) and A Little Lake Music (Kindle Vella), that don't have exactly happy endings. But they aren't exactly unhappy, either. I leave it up to you to decide which they are.)

If any of this sounds interesting or you wish to check out my other books and short fiction, you can find me at http://www.FlorenceWitkop.com